THE GANG OF FOUR
Kung-fooey to the Rescue

THE GANG OF FOUR
Kung-fooey to the Rescue

by Yaacov Peterseil

ST. HELIER, JERSEY

Original hard cover edition published in 1986
Revised and updated soft cover edition published in 1995
Copyright © 1995 by Yaacov Peterseil

Cover Art: Chana Navon
Illustrations: Jacky Yarchi
ISBN: 965-483-009-4

Published by PITSPOPANY PRESS

Printed in Hungary

To my delicious children:
Tehila
Gedalia
Shlomo
Nachum
Tiferet
Temima
Yosef
Todahya
Tanya
They keep me constantly in touch with the world of kids.

To my dear wife, Tamar, who manages to put up with my occasional childishness. She is a special person who makes all of us feel special.

And to my lovely mother, who made my childhood a joy to remember.

Contents

Chapter 1

Secret Message

Isaac discovered the message quite by accident. At least he assumed it was a message of some sort. He hoped it wasn't one of those top secret confidential-type messages coming from the army or, God forbid, from the President's office right up the block. Why, oh why, had he tried to break his father's secret code? He was in for it this time — and how!

"Uh-oh," he muttered out loud, "if I've tapped into the President's computer then who knows what they'll do to me. It may be too late already. Oh, no! They probably think I know whatever it is I'm not supposed to know and now that they know it, they'll come looking for me...arrest me...lock me up...bring spy charges.... Oh, no!"

By this time Isaac, who was all of 10 years old, had worked himself up into such a state that he was sure the apartment house was surrounded, and that there were men outside his father's study who had orders to shoot to kill.

"But it's not my fault!" he shouted to no one in particular, although he secretly hoped the police would hear him and take pity.

"I swear!" he continued to yell, at times at the computer in front of him, at times at the ceiling. "I swear I don't know about the secret! I never knew about the secret! And I promise it is still a secret!"

With that, Isaac put his head down on the keyboard and started to cry.

"Hey, Izzy," called Isaac's sister, Ruth, from outside the study. "If you've got a secret it sure is the loudest secret I ever heard. Why don't you let me in and share this secret you don't know?"

Isaac jumped out of his father's chair and raced across the room to open the door. Then he stopped.

"Is there anyone else out there, Ruth?" he called, his ear pressed against the door.

"Anyone else? Of course there is," answered Ruth, smiling to herself, "I've got the President of Israel out here. We both want to hear your great secret which, of course, you don't know." She was having trouble controlling her laughter. But to Isaac her half-laughs sounded just like the noise armed guards might make as they waited on the other side of the door.

"Oh, no! Just as I thought," he whispered to himself. "Ruth," he shouted through the door, "tell the President I'm sorry. I'm coming out now. Don't shoot!"

Slowly, Isaac opened the door and walked out, his hands above his head, expecting to see the whole Israeli army in front of him. But all he saw was his sister laughing hysterically and saying, over and over again, "You are definitely the funniest, Izzy, the funniest."

Isaac put down his hands.

"You were just kidding?" he cried. "Just kidding?"

"What are you talking about?" Ruth gasped, trying hard to catch her breath. "You expected to see the President of Israel here? Are you crazy? Did you really...no, not even you, Izzy, could be that silly." And, once again, she began to laugh.

"Oh yeah," snickered Isaac, clearly embarrassed. "Well, you laugh now, but wait until you see what I found. I can hardly believe it myself. Look!" He held out the message in front of her.

Ruth took the computer printout and looked at it carefully. It was certainly a message of some sort, and it sounded like a secret message, but from the President's office? Preposterous!

"Look, Izzy," she said, more sensitive now to her younger brother's situation, "it sure looks like a message. But how did you get it? When did it come over the computer? How was —?"

"Am I disturbing anything here?" asked Jacob, Ruth's twin. "I was studying math in my room, but this sounds a lot more interesting. Hey, Izzy, if the President thinks your message is really good, I may give up seventh grade altogether and work on secret messages full time, hah-hah."

"Jake," Ruth said sternly, "this is no time for your humor, such as it is. This is serious and Izzy may be in real trouble if we don't help him out. He just got a secret message through Dad's computer and he's worried he may get into trouble. Right, Izzy?"

"Yeah. And you know what, Jake, I think this is a really important message. But I don't know what happened to make it come out of Dad's printer. All I did was try a new — "

"Don't tell me," Jake interrupted, "after Dad warned you not to play with the computer you did it anyway?"

"Well," Izzy shot back, trying hard to defend himself, "I think I just about broke his code, wise guy. I had it just about figured out when this —"

"Cut it out you two," Ruth broke in. "We'll help you, Izzy. But chances are, the people who wrote this message don't even know you have it. Why don't we just tear it up, or give it to the police if you think it's important?"

"No way!" answered Isaac. "This is my secret message and I'm going to find out who sent it and what it means, all by myself."

"Without us?" shouted Ruth, horrified that her younger brother would even think of uncovering a secret without her.

"Come on, Izzy," Jake added, putting his arms around both his brother and sister, "you know we three make a great team. Remember the time Benjy got lost and we found him? Remember? Now that was team work. That's what we need now."

"What are you talking about, Jake?" Ruth asked, suddenly in the mood for a good fight. "Don't you remember how we spread out looking for Benjy, and each of us got lost? We found him, all right, when they took us to the lost and found. We were all lost until Mom and Dad came for us."

"Gee, you're picky!" Jake answered, taking his hand off Ruth's shoulder. "And anyway, whose side are you on? Remember, we're supposed to be trying to convince Izzy here to let us help him."

Then, looking at Izzy, Jake smiled. "Remember the Three Musketeers, all for one and one for all! That's us!"

"More like the Three Stooges," a little voice piped in. Of course, it was Benjy, fresh from watching a new kung-fu movie on the VCR in the living room. Benjy loved karate and, along with his older brothers and sister, took karate lessons twice a week in downtown Jerusalem. Naturally, being all of six years old, he knew very few of the more advanced steps the older children had mastered, but he could shout make-believe Korean commands with the best of them. Even as he talked, he would wave his hands and dance around as though warding off some terrible attackers.

"Ho-Cha! Ah-Zhoong!" he shouted, chopping imaginary villains in half and kicking the air around him. "Whadaya guys talking about?"

"Well, if it isn't Kung-fooey himself," laughed Isaac, who was forever teasing his younger brother.

"Izzy found a secret message, Benjy," Ruth solemnly explained, "and we're going to help him figure it out."

"Oh, can I help? Please? Pretty please? Come on, let me help. Chook-Chow! I'll get 'em, whoever they are, right in the eye. Pow! Please let me help!" begged Benjy.

"Are you kidding?" Jake asked. "How can you help

with a secret? You'll just blabber it to Mom and Dad. Or, worse, lose it somewhere."

"Whadaya mean lose it?" Benjy asked angrily. "I don't even have it. I don't even know what it is. Please, you gotta let me help. Please, Ruthy. Please?" Benjy knew he had the most leverage with his sister.

"Well, Benjy," Ruth began, "I don't know. It depends on your attitude. And Jake's right, you always tell. And you're afraid of the dark. And — "

"Wait!" interrupted Benjy, seeing an opening. "What does being afraid of the dark have to do with it?"

"Well," continued Ruth, "if we have to look for the meaning of the secret message in a dark place, or, if the time comes and we have to go out at night, you'll be afraid."

"I will not. I promise!" protested Benjy, starting to cry a little.

"Wait one second," Isaac suddenly said. "I found the secret and I decide who helps me discover its meaning."

"But I thought you wanted me to help you, Izzy?" Ruth asked, obviously hurt by Isaac's challenge to her leadership.

"Hey, me too," Jake added.

"What about me?" whined Benjy.

Isaac thought for a moment, and then smiled. "Okay, you can all help, but remember, it's my secret."

"Okay, okay," agreed Ruth, "but first we need to go over the facts, and make a plan."

"A good plan," Jake added.

"A super great plan," said Benjy, not to be outdone.

Chapter 2
MULTICOP

The Gold family had arrived in Israel just four months earlier. Besides Simon and his wife, Naomi, there were the twins, Jacob and Ruth (age twelve), Isaac (age ten), Benjamin (age six), Rebecca (age three), Rachel (age one), and, as the saying goes, "one more in the oven," due in about three weeks.

Naomi Gold had always planned to give her children Biblical names so that when they finally moved to Israel (as she always knew they would), the children would feel more at home. It was a bit of a disappointment for her to find that some of their Israeli friends were called "Sammy," "Jackie" and "Danny."

Within the family unit almost every child had his or her own "special" name. Jacob was Jake, Ruth was Ruthy, Isaac was Izzy, Rebecca was Bekka or Becky, and Rachel was...Rachel. The children had already decided that the unborn baby's nickname would be "Joe," if it turned out to be a boy, and "Jo," if it was a girl.

Simon Gold was a cryptologist. In the United States he worked for the government, setting up codes for millions of messages that the government sent when it didn't want anyone to know what was going on — which was most of the time. Mr. Gold was an expert in creating new codes that were just about unbreakable.

While he was finishing his doctorate in linguistics, the study of how languages are related to each other, he submitted a paper on the possibility of combining the best traits of certain languages to form a totally new language. One of his professors, who was working on a coding problem for the government, saw immediately that Simon's theory might be useful to them. He sent Simon's paper to a certain Pentagon official for review. Before long Simon was given a large grant by the government in order to do research in the field of cryptology. Two years later he presented MULTICOP, which stood for Multi-Language Tactical Coding Program. MULTICOP quickly, and quietly, revolutionized the secret coding business.

Like many works of genius, however, it took a genius to understand how MULTICOP worked. To program the system you had to be fluent in Chinese, Hebrew and English, and have a working knowledge of Esperanto.

The government gave the entire project "Top Secret" status. Because of Simon's special "Top Secret" clearance, those he worked with began to call him "Topper," a nickname that stuck with him wherever he went. Eventually, other countries heard of MULTICOP (who ever heard of a state secret remaining a secret for long?) and wanted to use its technology. The State Department, however, had spent too much time and money to allow any government, even a friendly one, to learn the secrets of MULTICOP. The Cold War may have frozen over, but that didn't mean other countries, especially in the Middle East, wouldn't try to use MULTICOP for their own sinister purposes — if they could get it, and understand it.

Only tiny Israel's request for the MULTICOP system had been okayed. No one knew exactly why, except Topper. He was there under cover. Everyone, including his family, believed this was the long-awaited vacation he had promised them, a year in Israel. But his real mission was to help Israel monitor the Iraq-Iran-Syria airwaves.

So, twice a week, Mr. Gold went to Israel's top secret defense facilities near Tel Aviv to work on setting up a MULTICOP system which would work only — and this was the key American demand — when linked up with the U.S. MULTICOP system. This meant that Israel would need clearance from the State Department before it could use its MULTICOP system. But that was all right with the Israelis. They believed they would figure out how to overcome any obstacles that the United States might put in their way. Topper was there to make sure they could not.

The rest of the week Mr. Gold worked on his computer at home, using a direct link-up with the strategic computers in Tel Aviv. There was, of course, a special set of codes for this link-up and it was Isaac's personal goal to break this code and show his father what a great computer "hack" he was.

The Gold family lived in Jerusalem in a nice five-bedroom apartment on Jabotinsky Street, down the block from the President's House. They were able to get their apartment with the help of their aunt, Shoshanna, a personal secretary to the President, and one of the best-connected Israelis around. "Proteksia," the art of knowing the right person to help you, was a major factor in making life in Israel enjoyable, and not just livable. With Aunt Shoshanna's help, the Golds were able to accomplish in four months what took others over a year (and then some) to do.

The four oldest Gold children had become closer than ever during their stay in Israel. They took public transportation to school, together; went out for lunch almost every day, together; and helped each other with everyday problems. Ruth made it her own special mission to keep a watchful eye on Benjy, while acting as self-appointed leader of the others.

Mrs. Gold had her hands full with the little ones. Her years as a successful family therapist and social worker were being put to good use in Israel. Every day a new problem would crop up, and every day she would be there to help solve it, often anticipating the needs of her children. Simon sometimes made fun of his wife's preoccupation with their family problems, calling Naomi their "in-house, full-time social worker." But secretly, he admired her ability to confront each new situation head-on, and when it came to a discussion about how to handle any child, he always gave in to her.

Unlike Israeli families, whose main meal was lunch, the Gold family got together each evening for a traditional American supper. When Simon or Naomi felt things were not going as smoothly as they would like, it was Simon's job to begin the meal by asking, "Well, who wants to start by telling me their day?" This question, according to Naomi, was designed to make self-expression by the children easier and more natural.

Perhaps it did. Sometimes.

This evening, however, it was not so simple.

"Well, who wants to start by telling me their day?" Mr. Gold began, innocently enough. Usually, each child would talk about school, or friends, or problems of a not-too-personal nature. Not that any of them wanted to discuss these things. But they knew that if they didn't say something, Mrs. Gold would immediately imagine the worst and start grilling them, in detail, about everything they had done that day, until she found the reason for their silence. So, each child automatically prepared a little something to say, usually not enough to arouse their mother's curiosity, but not so little that they would run the risk of being cross-examined.

Actually, Mr. Gold was not very curious by nature. After a hard day's work he would have been happy to eat his meal in peace, without necessarily knowing his children's everyday problems. But, if it was good for his children to "come clean," well, then, he would play his part. Of course, he would have liked to get it all over with before the soup, but, often as not, the kids would want to talk right through to the main course, which they hardly ever ate.

"Jacob, why don't you begin. What happened today?" Mr. Gold prompted.

"Oh, nothing much. I got an 80 on my history test and a 90 on the Talmud quiz. My friend, Yehuda, showed me how to do a head shot in soccer, and I almost had to beat up a tenth-grader."

"Fine, Jacob, those sound like great marks," Mr. Gold said, half listening, hoping to be able to finish the grilling quickly so he could eat the main course without interruptions. Tonight it was turkey schnitzel and corn-on-the-cob, one of his favorites.

No such luck.

"What do you mean, you 'almost had to beat up a tenth-grader?'" Mrs. Gold repeated, frowning at her husband.

"Yes, Jacob, what do you mean you almost beat him up?" Mr. Gold quickly spoke up, taking his cue from his wife and hoping his son had a good, short answer.

"Well, he kept getting in my way. He said I wasn't allowed to pass him. Finally, I said that if he didn't stand aside I would go through him."

"And did you hit him?" Mrs. Gold asked.

"Yes, did you hit him?" Mr. Gold echoed.

"Well, not exactly," Jacob mumbled, starting to feel uncomfortable. "I told him he was stupid and ran around him. Being fat and slow, he just shouted at me."

"And do you think you did the right thing?" asked his mother.

"Sure," he answered, sounding less sure by the minute.

"Topper," Mrs. Gold turned to her husband, "please tell him what he did wrong. I'm tired of telling him the same thing all the time."

"Wrong?" Mr. Gold repeated, trying to think of the right answer. He vaguely remembered how his wife hated name-calling. Of course. That had to be it.

"Jacob," he said, confident that he was on the right track, "next time a situation like this comes up just stomp on the guy's foot and head for the hills. There's no need to call people names. Haven't we taught you that by now?" he concluded, glancing at Naomi for approval.

"No, no, no! Not at all," Naomi scolded, clearly upset.

"Jacob, you shouldn't call people names — or fight. That's stupid. You should have reasoned with him. Talked to him so you could find out why he's picking on you. First, always reason with your enemy. And, if that doesn't work — "

"Then I'll stomp on him like Dad said, and run away," Jacob quickly stuck in, smiling at his father.

Mr. Gold wished he could make himself disappear.

"And, if that doesn't work," Mrs. Gold repeated, louder now, making it clear she was ignoring his remark for his own good, "then call for help. Certainly a teacher or another adult will come and help you."

"Yes, Mom," said Jacob, realizing none too soon that it was a losing battle.

"Now it's your turn, Ruth," Mr. Gold announced, knowing he had to make good after his last paternal blunder. The turkey schnitzel seemed a long way from ever filling his empty stomach.

"Well," Ruth began, "I know I shouldn't be speaking bad about anyone, but this girl Esther just keeps getting on my nerves in school. She is always making fun of me and she tells the other girls not to play with me. And you know what else? Yesterday at the assembly everyone was willing to move over and give me some room to sit down except ugly-face Esther." Ruth leaned back hard against her chair. She was glad to have gotten all this off her chest, but a little unsure of her parents' reaction. She glanced at her mother.

"I think I understand," Mr. Gold replied. He felt confident that this time his answers would be on the money. "First, don't call people names." He knew he'd gotten that one right. "And next, remember we've explained to you how difficult it is when you enter a new school. Children can be cruel sometimes. Esther may be jealous of all the attention some of the other girls are giving you. She may feel you don't want to play with her, or she may not even understand you so well when you speak Hebrew. Maybe try to be friends with a non-Israeli," Mr. Gold advised, happy to have solved this problem without his wife's help.

"But Dad," Ruth cried out, "Esther is American! She came here when we did. And I speak English to her!" Ruth was clearly upset now.

"Oh!" Simon said, wondering what else could go wrong. "Well, if that's the case, Ruth," he offered, hoping somehow to relieve the rising tension, "then maybe you should do like Jacob — stomp on her foot and run away. Hah, hah, hah, just joking."

The other kids laughed, but Ruth didn't find it funny at all.

"Oh, Dad," she shouted, "I'm not in the mood for any of your jokes."

"Ruth," Mrs. Gold said softly, coming to her husband's rescue, "if I were you I'd ignore Esther or, if you find it too hard to do that then next time she says something to you that isn't nice just go over and ask her straight out why she doesn't like you. You'd be surprised at how success-ful a move like that can be."

"Exactly what I was thinking," Mr. Gold said, actually thinking of the, by now, burnt schnitzel and overcooked corn.

"And now you, Isaac. What's new with you?" Mr. Gold asked, hoping for a one-word answer.

"Me? Nothing, nothing at all," Isaac blurted out. "I promise. Nothing new. Didn't even touch your computer today. Didn't read any messages or letters. Nope, nothing much happened today all right." Isaac's face was flushed and his eyes kept darting back and forth from his father to his mother.

"Are you all right, Isaac?" Mrs. Gold asked, genuinely concerned. "You certainly seem nervous. Is there some-thing you want to tell us? Something you'd rather say in private?"

"Me? Private?" Isaac repeated, his face getting redder by the minute. "No, not a thing. Just a quiet day all around. No messages. No letters. Nothing private. Just a typical day."

"Isaac," Mrs. Gold began, "I get the feel — "

"Now Naomi, stop it," Simon interrupted, sensing that this was not the time for any major revelations. "Issac's just hungry, like we all are. Right, kids?" he asked, as they all nodded their approval, especially Isaac. "And anyway, Naomi, if it's private, ask him privately," Mr. Gold concluded, happy to have ended the conversation and aware that only one more cross-examination lay between him and his meal.

"Benjy, what have you got to say for yourself?" he quickly asked.

"Can I pass my turn to Bekka?"

"No, I'm afraid you're the last one dear," his mother said with a smile.

"Okay, then nothing happened today," Benjy announced. "Let's eat!"

"Sounds good to me," seconded Mr. Gold, getting ready for the feast.

"Not so fast, Benjy," Mrs. Gold warned. "First Isaac, now you. There's something fishy going on and I want to know what it is. Right now!"

"Well, Mom, it's like this," began Benjy, as all his brothers and sisters turned their stares at him.

"I've got a secret which I can't tell you," Benjy slyly answered, enjoying the way his siblings were squirming in their chairs.

"Come on, Benjy," Mr. Gold almost begged. "Tell your mother the secret or the food is going to burn to death."

"Great!" answered Benjy. "I love well-done food."

"I'm going to make you well-done, if you don't answer your mother right now," his father declared, losing his temper.

"Okay, okay. The secret is," and here Benjy stopped to clear his throat and check the horror on the faces of Jake, Ruth and Izzy, "the secret is that I know where babies come from."

"What?" practically everyone at the table said in unison. Jake, Ruth and Izzy visibly breathed a sigh of relief, but they too were curious as to how Benjy planned to explain himself.

"Yes," he continued, pointing to his mother's swollen stomach. "Babies sit in the mother's stomach listening through the belly-button until they're ready to fall out and then the father takes the mother to the hospital where a doctor catches the baby when it falls out, so it won't break its little head," Benjy concluded with a smile. The other children laughed loudly, almost hysterically.

"That's not bad, Benjy," his father admitted. "Except for a few details you're pretty close. Now, let's eat!"

The rest of dinner was short but delicious.

After the meal the four older children met in Ruth's room to go over the message and decide on a plan.

"Benjy," Isaac began, looking sternly at his younger brother, "you really fooled us there. But you try giving me a heart attack again and I'll stuff you into Dad's computer."

"Yeah, Fooey," Jake added in mock anger, "but you came through in the end. You did pretty good for a little squirt."

"That's right, Benjy," Ruth declared, "you were great. And all this shows, as I've told you boys time and time again, that we four can be a great team."

"No," Benjy said, "let's not be a team. Let's be a gang, like in the movies. A good gang against the bad gangs. And we win, naturally. Wang! Bam! Boom!" Benjy started kicking and chopping the air.

"That's not bad, not bad at all," Ruth applauded.

"Thanks, Ruthy," Benjy answered, sure she was complimenting his Kung-fu movements.

"Yes, Benjy, a great idea," she continued, not even hearing the painful "oh" from Benjy as he realized she was only interested in his suggestion.

"Yeah," Isaac's eyes lit up as he thought of the possibilities. "A secret gang! A gang of four against the bad guys who wrote that message."

"If the bad guys wrote that message," Ruth warned, throwing a little cold water on all their excitement. "Remember, you thought it might be from someone in the Israeli government."

"Yeah," Isaac thought for a moment, then waved her comment aside. "But now I think — I know — it's the bad guys. And the gang of four is going to get them."

"Okay," agreed Ruth, enthusiastic once again, "I've got a great idea. Let's get the old Saracen sword and use it to make a pact." Jake ran to his room and plucked the sword off its stand on the wall. When he returned they all put one hand around the sword's hilt.

"We solemnly promise," Ruth intoned, "that we will not rest until we find out who the bad guys are and what the message means." They all nodded. But no one knew what to do next.

"Yea gang of four!" Ruth suddenly shouted.

"Yea gang of four!" they all yelled.

And the gang of four was born.

"Let's be a gang, like in the movies. A good gang against the
bad gangs. And we win, naturally. Wang! Bam! Boom!"

Chapter 3
Chung! Chuk! Chu!

Lemme see it, come on, Izzy, lemme see it, pleeeease," Benjy begged, jumping up and down and slicing through the air with his hands, fighting his imaginary foe.

"Yes, Izzy," Ruth added, "we've got to see the message and analyze it before we know what to do."

"I'll bet that when we go over it, we'll find there is no message," Jake teased. "Just some mixed up sentences you got through Dad's computer, which you shouldn't have been playing with in the first place. Anyway, if it is a message, why aren't you letting us go over it ourselves?"

"Okay, okay, just wait a minute," Izzy said, holding up his hands and walking around his room like a man who suddenly realizes he is in charge. He liked the feeling.

"First we've got to settle two things," he commanded. "A, no one besides the four of us is allowed to see the message, and B, if there is any reward, I get most of it." Slowly, he looked at each one in turn and then sat down as if to say, "them's the rules, take it or leave it."

"Isaac Gold!" Ruth screamed, "How can you talk like that? We're all in this together, and if there is any reward we'll divide it equally," she declared, reaffirming her position as boss of the gang.

"That's not fair," he pouted, his feelings of superiority slowly fading. "At least let me have more than the flying kata-klutz there," he whined, pointing at Benjy. "After all, I found the message!"

"Okay, boys," Ruth said, with a wink at Jake, "if that's the way Izzy wants to act, then let him have his message and his secret and we'll just leave." With that, she took Benjy, who kept saying, "no, no, no," with one hand, and Jake with the other, and started walking out of the room.

"One second, Ruth," Isaac whispered, knowing at last that his brief moment of control was over. "I have an even better idea. Let's give the reward money to Mom and Dad for a house. Then, maybe we can get a swimming pool."

"Sounds good to me," Jake cautiously answered, waiting to see if his sister agreed.

"Okay," Ruth nodded.

"Okay," Benjy echoed. "We'll buy them a new house...and I get a new bike," he quietly added, hoping no one would notice his little personal touch.

"Quiet, squirt," Jake snapped as Benjy kicked out in disappointment. "Now, Izzy, let's see the message."

Izzy had been waiting for just this moment. Like all good detectives, Isaac had hidden the message where no one would ever find it. Buried in his closet — where it was impossible to find anything anyway — in an old shoe box was his old collection of Series Five Garbage Pail Kids.

And, pressed between his two favorite cards — Neck Ty, showing a bald child hanging himself, and Batty Barney, showing the same child hanging upside down with a blood-sucking bat body — was the message.

"Well, here it is!" Isaac announced as he made his way out of the closet. Trailing behind him was an assortment of clothes and about two dozen bottle caps, obviously left over from another "collection."

"Congratulations for getting out of there alive," laughed Jake, "It smells like someone or something else was not so lucky."

"Yeah," giggled Benjy. "Now I know what happened to the green salamander I lost last year." Izzy's beaming face grew dull.

"Okay, boys," warned Ruth, sensing the joking had gone far enough, "Izzy did the right thing by hiding the message. Now open it up, Izzy, and we'll read the letter together."

Carefully, as though opening a very old and valuable document, Izzy unfolded the message and read it out loud.

WARNING! WARNING!
READ AND DESTROY AT ONCE!
FROM: CELL LEADER DEMHCA
TO: COMMANDER BUKAY

PRIMARY TARGET LOCATED STOP
HOSTAGE ONLY STOP ATTACK SECONDARY
AIR TARGET STOP SELF-DESTRUCT AS

DIRECTED STOP STRIKE DATE: 12TH OF
RAMADAN STOP HOSTAGE PICK UP AGREED
TIME AT SEA STOP
ALLAH ACHBAR!

"Wow!" Jake exclaimed, barely able to contain his excitement. "This is the real thing, Izzy. We'd better get this to the police right away."

"I don't know, Jake," Ruth said, weighing their options. "If this is a government message, then we may really be in for it when they find out we intercepted. But, then again, if it really is a terrorist message, maybe we should go to the police. Of course, we could just throw it away and — "

"What?" Izzy yelped, afraid he was about to lose his claim to fame. "Are you crazy? If we know about the terrorists, then we have to do something!"

"Chung! Chuk! Chu! I think we should cut 'em up. Get the ninchucks, Jake, and we'll bash their bones in," Benjy advised.

"One second, boys. Let's think about this," Ruth continued, ignoring Benjy's battle cry. "We don't know when the 12th of Ramadan falls out, or even what it is. Maybe this is some old message and it, whatever it is, has already happened? And then there's always the chance that we may be able to pick up more messages which might clear the whole thing up. I say we wait another day and see if there is any more we can find out."

"As a matter of fact," Izzy said, "I purposely left the computer on to see if there would be any more messages. Maybe something came through while we were eating."

In a flash the gang ran to their father's computer. Three of them huddled over the computer's printer, leaving Benjy to stand guard. Sure enough, there was another message. It read simply:

MESSAGE RECEIVED

They took the printout to Izzy's room.

"Uh-oh," Izzy suddenly gulped.

"What's the matter, Izzy?" Ruth asked.

"I just thought of something terrible. It's possible that if our computer is receiving these messages, then whoever is really supposed to receive these messages is living right in this building!"

"Oh, no!" Jake moaned. "There must be dozens of families in this building. Who knows how many have a computer?"

"Dad knows," Izzy volunteered.

"What do you mean, Iz?" Ruth asked.

"Well," Izzy continued, "when Dad needed to set up the computer, he asked the tenants' organization in the building for permission to tap into the building's power supply. Dad told me that our computer was so strong that the tenants' organization insisted that Dad get permission from everyone in the building who had a computer."

"Okay then," Ruth said, "let's just ask Dad how many people have computers in this building, and who they are, and then we can check them out."

"What?" Isaac gasped. "And have Dad ask us why we

need to know. And possibly find out about my message. And how I got it when I wasn't supposed to be near his computer. Great! That will be curtains for me."

"Yeah," added Benjy, "and I won't have a new bicycle."

"Well, then what do we do?" asked Jake.

"Let me think," Ruth suggested, putting her index finger to her lips. "Wait! I've got it! It's simple. Until we know for sure whether there is something worth telling Dad and possibly getting Isaac into trouble for, we have to check things out ourselves. What we need is someone to ask Dad for the information we need. Someone who could confuse Dad enough so he wouldn't suspect what we're doing. Someone whom Dad would think is just being his old silly self."

All eyes turned to Benjy.

"No problem, gang," Benjy beamed, happy for the attention. "I'll just go to Dad and ask him who is sending us messages on his computer. Then I'll Wham! Chung! Kwow! Zonk 'em with my ninchucks. You guys can help too. Okay?"

"I can see the headlines now," Jake announced sarcastically.

KUNG-FOOEY STRIKES!

THOUSANDS KILLED WITH ONE BLOW!

FOOEY SAVES THE DAY!

Jake and Izzy started laughing.

"Yea, me!" yelled Benjy, starting another round of laughter.

"Boys!" commanded Ruth and everyone quickly stopped laughing. "That's better. Now, I think that if we tell Benjy what he should ask, and how, he could do it. Now, no more wisecracks."

"Fine," said Jake, "but we still have to make sure he understands what he's supposed to say."

"Okay. Don't worry. I'll remember," Benjy defended himself.

"What we basically have to know," Ruth said, "is the name of the head of the tenants' organization so we can try and get the names of everyone who has a computer."

"No problem," Benjy explained, "I'll just ask Dad the name of the tenants' organs. Okay?"

"Not organs," Isaac moaned, "organization. Tenants' organization. Somehow I don't think this is going to work."

"Come on, Izzy," Ruth tried to sound encouraging. "After we go over it a bit he'll be just fine. But Benjy, don't forget you have to ask a lot of other questions before you ask ours so that Dad won't suspect anything."

"Okay already. Bang! Wham! Kapow! No problem! Gimme the questions."

After almost an hour of rehearsing the major question and about half a dozen unrelated ones, Benjy seemed ready. His only real problem was remembering how to say tenants' organization.

Or so it seemed.

Chapter 4

Mr. Gevalt

Hi, Dad! Whatcha doing?"

Mr. Gold looked up from his papers and smiled as Benjy walked into his study.

"Hi, Benj. I'm a little busy now, unless you have something important you want to discuss."

"Oh," Benjy sighed, unsure as to whether he should start his shpiel or not. After a moment he decided to go ahead.

"Well, Dad, I need to ask you some questions for my project."

"What project, Benjy? You've got a project in first grade?" Mr. Gold tried to sound serious but a thin smile moved across his lips. Benjy had only just begun to learn to read and write in Hebrew and in English.

"Sure, Dad, of course I have a project," Benjy insisted.

"The teacher said I have to ask my father some questions and we'll discuss them in class. It's like telling a story." Benjy beamed. He was proud of himself for remembering, word for word, Ruth's instructions.

"But how do you take notes?" Mr. Gold asked.

Benjy pointed to his head and, smiling, said, "Kidneys, Dad, kidneys. Morah Devora, that's my teacher, wants us to memorize all the answers, so all you have to do is make sure I understand what you're saying and then I'll be able to tell the class."

"Okay, Benjy, shoot," his father said goodnaturedly.

"Pow!" Benjy yelled, pretending to shoot a gun and laughing. "Okay, here's the first question: When you were little were there any dinosaurs around? And if there were, how many?"

Simon Gold started to laugh, but seeing his son's serious expression, thought better of it.

"Er, interesting question, Benj. My generation missed the dinosaurs by a little, although you might want to ask your mother the same question. She might have seen a few," Mr. Gold added, wondering how his wife would handle their son's question.

"Yes," Benjy persisted, "but if there would have been dinosaurs in your time, how many would there have been?"

Mr. Gold, seeing he was not going to win, calmly answered, "Six. Plus one pregnant pterodactyl."

"See," Benjy jumped up, "I told you there were some!"

Mr. Gold looked a little dumbfounded. Benjy, meanwhile, was wondering whether to ask the important question, or wait until his father had answered a few more fake ones. So far everything was going according to plan.

Might as well give him the big one, he thought.

"Dad, one more question please."

"Okay, Benjy, but please make it quick, and simple. I must finish this work within the next few hours."

"Well, this is an easy question, Dad." Benjy took a deep breath, wondering to himself if his question was going to come out right. "Who is in charge of the tenants' organization?"

"What?" his father asked, hardly believing his ears.

"Didn't I say 'tenants' organization' right?" Benjy asked, fearing he had failed after all.

"No, Benjy, you said it fine. But why would you need to know such a thing for your project?"

Benjy was ready.

"Well," he began, "dinosaurs once lived together, right?"

"Yes," his father answered, curious as to how Benjy was going to explain himself.

"And people live together in apartment houses like this, right?"

His father nodded his head in agreement. Benjy searched his brain for the exact words Ruth had told him to say when, and if, he got this far.

"Well, then it's simple. Just like dinosaurs needed a boss to keep them together and make sure they wouldn't get on each other's nerves, so people need a boss to keep themselves together so they don't bother each other. Now," and here Benjy swallowed hard, "the boss of the dinosaurs was probably called Godzilla or something like that. And the boss of the people is called the guy in charge of the tenants' organization. And what I want for my project to be complete is his name so I can have the name of both bosses. Okay?"

Mr. Gold was silent for a moment, wondering what Benjy was talking about. He knew a "snow job" when he heard one.

"Benjamin," he began softly. Suddenly Benjy knew he was in trouble.

"Er, that's okay, Dad, no problem. I think I'll do a different project anyhow. Maybe on how babies go to the potty, or how to find lost baseball cards or something." Benjy took a tentative step backward toward the safety of the door. "See you later, Dad," he said, trying to smile as he turned to leave.

"Benjamin," his father said, a little louder and a little more menacingly. "Benjamin, who put you up to this and why do you want to know the name of the head of the tenants' organization?"

"Well, Dad, maybe — "

"Right now, Benjamin!" his father interrupted.

"Yes, okay, no problem. It's just that I promised not to tell and if Ruthy finds out I told she won't let me be part of the gang and then I won't know the secret and go out at night and find the bad guys and chop 'em good. Kapow! Kabang! Whoom!" He brought his fists down on the imaginary bad guys, all the while making his way closer and closer to the door.

"As usual, Benjy, I don't know what you're talking about," a very frustrated Mr. Gold scolded. "But, if this is just part of one of your crazy games, then okay, I'll tell you the name. His name is Jeff Golan."

Benjy couldn't believe it. There it was. The name.

"Oh, thank you, thank you, Dad. I promise — "

"Don't promise anything, Benjy," his father said, softening his tone. "Just don't lie to me again. Ask me whatever you want or better yet, tell that gang of yours to ask me instead of putting you up to it." Then, turning back to his work, Mr. Gold added, "Now go finish your game and tell the others, especially Ruth, that I'll want to speak to them at length later."

"No problem, Dad." Quick as a flash Benjy was outside the study and racing back to Izzy's room, where all the others were waiting.

"Well, how did it go, Benjy?" Isaac asked as soon as his brother walked into the room.

"No problem, guys," Benjy lied. "No problem at all. Dad told me the answer just like this." Benjy tried to snap his fingers, but couldn't so he karate-chopped the air.

"I don't know," Jake said, sensing there was more to this than Benjy was letting on. "You mean to tell me Dad believed all that stuff about dinosaurs and bosses and all that other junk?"

"Hey, Jake, I said no problem. Mucho easy," Benjy continued lying, wondering what they would do to him when they found out he had almost given away the secret.

"I told Dad exactly what you told me to say and he told me the name of the boss of the tenants' organization. His name is Ga...Ge...Go...." Benjy suddenly realized he didn't remember the name. He tried desperately to search through his vocabulary of Hebrew or Yiddish words that began with Ga, Ge, or Go.

"Well, come on," Izzy demanded. "Don't tell me you've forgotten the name already?"

"No, of course not. I was just fooling around." Benjy tried a sickly smile but no one else was smiling. He needed more time. But his time was up.

"The boss of the tenants' organization is...is... Mr. Gevalt," he announced with as much sincerity as he could muster.

"Gevalt!" exclaimed Jake, beginning to laugh. "Gevalt! But that's a Yiddish expression Dad uses. It means 'Oh, no!' or something like that. Are you sure the last name is Gevalt?"

"Of course I'm sure," Benjy answered confidently, knowing it was too late to back out now.

"You faker, you," Izzy mocked. "You forgot the name didn't you? Didn't you? Come on, admit it."

"I did not, dumdum."

"Liar!"

"Idiot!"

"Pimple!"

"Goulash!"

No doubt the battle of words would have continued until the first blow was struck, were it not for Ruth. She had been quiet throughout the debriefing of Benjy. But now she spoke up.

"Boys! Boys!!" she shouted. Silence prevailed. "Boys, forget all this silliness. All we have to do is go downstairs and look at the mailboxes to find out if there is a Mr. Gevalt and which apartment he lives in."

"Great idea, Ruth," Benjy applauded, glad to have been saved, for the moment. "Maybe I should stay up here and check — "

"What's the matter, Fooey, afraid the Gevalt family has disappeared?" Izzy chided.

"Don't worry, Benjy, the rest of us believe you," Ruth assured him. "You did a great job. Boy, you must have really fooled Dad. I hope he won't get mad at you when this is all over."

"I'm sure he won't," Benjy quietly answered, deciding at the same time to wait a few days before telling Ruth that their father wanted to talk to her.

Ruth led the gang of four down the stairs to the first floor (the elevator was broken, as usual). Once there, they looked at all the mailboxes but couldn't find anyone named Gevalt.

"Hey Benjy, are you sure about the name?" Jake asked. "There's nothing even close here."

"Well, I'm pretty sure the name was Gevalt," came the lame answer, "and I'm positive it started with a G." Benjy saw Izzy's I-told-you-so expression. So did everyone else.

"That's just great," continued Jake. "Let's see now, there are three names that begin with G. Grosky, Golan, and...oh, no, another Golan!"

"Well," Ruth said, "it makes sense to start with the Golan families. Chances are good they're the ones we're looking for."

"Yeah, that's it!" Benjy exclaimed. "Golan. That's the name! Golan!"

"But Benjy," Izzy solemnly suggested, "won't the Gevalt family be upset when they find out they don't live here any more? And boy will they be angry when they find out they don't even exist! Eh, Kung-fooey?"

Benjy looked down at the tips of his shoes.

"Forget it, Izzy," Ruth ordered. "Let's get going."

Silently, they began the climb to the third floor, and the first Golan family.

Chapter 5
Killer Poodle

Okay, we're here," announced Jake as they stood in front of 3C where George Golan lived. "What do we do now?" he asked.

"Simple," whispered Ruth, a bit nervous but trying hard to appear confident in front of her brothers. "We'll ring the bell, and when he opens it we'll introduce ourselves and tell him we heard he's head of the tenants' organization."

"Great," Jake whispered back. "But what are you going to say when he asks us what we want?"

"Just that we have a school project which he could help us with. Then slowly, using the same methods that worked on Dad, I'll get the answers we need from him," she hoped.

"Okay, you win," Jake responded, happy he didn't have to lead this fishing expedition. "But somehow I don't think it will be as easy as you think."

"You worry too much, Jake," Ruth smiled, worried herself.

"Oh Ruthy," Benjy was raising his hand.

"What is it Benjy? And stop raising your hand. This isn't class."

"Oh, right. But I think I should tell you not to ask him about dinosaurs or things like that. I don't think it will work on anyone but Dad. But, just in case he gives you any trouble, I'll karate him. Pow! Bam! Zonk!" Benjy declared.

"Thanks for the advice, Benj," Ruth said. "Now, why don't you ring the bell?"

"Sure," Benjy happily agreed. "Watch this!" With a swift movement, Benjy hit the bell hard, using a knife hand attack. The bell rang, but not as loud as Benjy's "Ouch!" or his stomping up and down in pain.

"Great move, Kung-fooey," Izzy said. "Now why don't you kick the door down, preferably with your head."

Before anyone could laugh, a fierce, blood-curdling growl from the other side of the door blasted into the hallway.

Everyone froze.

"Wa—well, gang," Izzy stammered, "no—no one seems to be home. We can come back later. Much later."

"Wait! I hear something," Jake reported, pressing his ear against the door.

"I hear it too," Izzy agreed. "That's why I want to leave."

"No, I mean I heard someone say 'I'm coming!'"

"I think I heard it too," Ruth seconded. "Ring the bell again, Benjy."

"Are you kidding? Izzy's right. Nobody said anything except that wild animal in there. And all I heard him say was 'I'm hungry!'"

Ruth rang the bell herself. The dog growled again, a little softer this time, and all of them could clearly hear a voice say, "Coming! Just one second."

The door opened a crack.

"Are you kids afraid of dogs?" a man's voice asked.

Bravely, Jake, Ruth and Izzy said no.

Benjy, positioned well behind the others, yelled "yes!"

"Well, don't worry about this dog. He's big, but he's harmless," the voice on the other side of the door assured them. "Just let him smell your hand and he'll be your friend."

Slowly, the door opened and a giant black poodle, almost Benjy's height, confronted the gang.

"Now, each of you, give him your hand."

First Jake, then Ruth, and then Izzy carefully extended a hand and gave the dog a chance to smell it. Benjy stayed back. Way back.

"Now you, young man," the owner of the dog said.

"Could—couldn't he just smell my shoes?" a very nervous Benjy asked.

"That won't do at all, young man. Now, don't be afraid, he's eaten already. Just give him your hand." Very, very slowly, Benjy put his hand out in front of the poodle. The dog sniffed it for a second and then licked it with his long wet, pink tongue.

"Hey, gang," Benjy beamed with delight, "he really likes me."

"It seems he does. But let me introduce myself. I'm George Golan. Why don't you all come in and have something to drink? You must be the new children from the seventh floor."

"Yes," Ruth answered. "I'm Ruth Gold. This is Jacob, Isaac and Benjamin. Thank you for inviting us in but we just want to ask you a question."

"Yeah," Benjy interrupted, feeling more secure now that the dog was his friend. "Do you own a tenants' organization, a computer, or know any secrets like we know?" he shot out.

"Quiet, squirt!" Izzy hissed. He tried to push Benjy away, but the dog growled and Izzy thought better of it.

"I'm sorry, Mr. Golan," Ruth apologized. "Benjy has such a vivid imagination. Actually, we did want to know if you are the head of the tenants' organization?"

"No, not at all. But what is this about computers, Benjy?" Mr. Golan called out. Benjy, happy to have a grown-up pay attention to him, moved closer and started to say, "Well, we found a sec —" Jake's hand covered Benjy's mouth. Ruth quickly apologized again for bothering Mr. Golan. Everyone said goodbye to the dog and the man, and started for the next floor where Golan #2 lived.

George Golan watched the gang as they headed upstairs. He was deep into his own thoughts as he quietly closed the door.

"Are you crazy, Benjy?" Izzy blared as soon as he heard Mr. Golan close the door.

"Yeah, what are you trying to do? Get us killed?" Jake added, visibly upset. "What if he was the spy or terrorist or who knows what? Do you want him to know we know anything?"

Slowly, the door opened and a giant black poodle, almost Benjy's height, confronted the gang.

"You almost got us into real trouble there, Benjy," Ruth scolded. But, seeing the tears well up in Benjy's eyes, she started to feel guilty. After all, she thought to herself, he's only six.

"You know what, Benjy," she said out loud, speaking in her motherly voice, "it really doesn't matter. We know he's not the head of the tenants' organization now, so it must be the second Golan. Now we'll get some useful information."

"I don't care!" Benjy yelled, crying at the same time. "It's not only your secret, it's mine too! And I can tell it to whoever I want. I don't need to listen to you any more. I can do what I want to!"

Then, before anyone could stop him, Benjy ran up the stairs.

"Let him go, boys," Ruth ordered. "He'll go home. We can talk to him later."

"But won't he blab to everyone?" Izzy asked.

"No," Ruth answered, "I think he's just angry. He knows he shouldn't have said anything before but he doesn't know how to handle his guilt. We all jumped on him too hard. But I'm sure he'll get over it."

"Boy, Ruth," Jake said, admiringly, "you sound more and more like Mom every day."

"That's because you guys act more and more like Benjy every day," retorted Ruth, secretly proud of the compliment she'd been given.

As they reached the landing of the fourth floor, a woman stepped out of 4K, the apartment they were coming to visit.

"Excuse me," Ruth quietly asked, "are you Mrs. Golan?"

"Yes, I am," she answered, locking the door and turning toward the children.

"Great," continued Ruth, "we want to ask you a question. Are you or your husband head of the tenants' organization?"

"Yes, my husband is. He'll be back in half an hour, if you care to come back. I'm sure he'll be happy to talk to you then."

"Great!" Ruth exclaimed. "We'll be back."

The children slowly began climbing the stairs to the seventh floor. As they approached the sixth they heard a terrific scream.

"Help! Help! Jake, help me!"

"It's Benjy!" shouted Jake. Without waiting for the others, he bounded up the stairs until he reached the next landing. Once there, he could barely believe his eyes. Benjy was fighting, tooth and nail, with a stranger. The man kept trying to lift Benjy. But every time the stranger got near Benjy, the boy kicked him with all his might. While Benjy missed most of the time, his attacker was learning to keep his distance. Then, suddenly, the man took out a knife, its long blade gleaming in the dim light of the stairwell.

"Boh iti, oh tamut kahn!" (Come with me, or you die here!) he spat between clenched teeth, coming closer and closer with the knife. "Maher!" (Quickly!) he commanded.

Jake saw his little brother freeze with fear. With a loud ear-splitting cry he kicked hard and high, hitting the stranger in the shoulder and throwing him off balance. The man slammed against a wall, momentarily dazed. Wasting no time, Jake delivered a devastating side-kick, knocking the knife out of the attacker's hand. The knife fell with a clang. The attacker jumped for it and Jake punched him in the back, hard, with all his might, letting out a short, violent breath of air at the same time, as he had been taught in karate class. The stranger yelled, grabbed the knife and half-ran, half-fell down the steps, scattering Ruth and Izzy who had just reached the landing.

Ruth and Izzy regained their balance and raced toward Jake who was shaking, barely able to stand. Benjy, however, had caught his second wind. He was feeling just fine. In fact, he was great.

"Gang! Gang!" he shouted. "Did you guys miss the greatest fight ever. Jake and I just beat up about fifteen terrorists. Pow! Bam! Kapow!" Benjy exhibited some of his fancy footwork. "We shmeared 'em. He kicked 'em high and I karated their toes. Then, when they tried to get me with their knives and machetes, we kicked them out of their hands, elbowed them in the guts, and ripped out their throats. Why, we — "

Izzy had to physically hold down his younger brother who was actively fighting off at least 10 attackers simultaneously.

"Easy, Kung-fooey," Izzy said, trying hard to restrain Benjy. "Before you kill anyone else, let's find out what *really* happened."

By this time, other people in the building, who had

heard the commotion, came running out of their apartments. Ruth grabbed Jake, and Izzy had to just about carry the karate-chopping Benjy, as they quickly made their way back to their apartment.

Once inside, they rushed to the computer room. There was Mr. Gold, busy typing instructions on the keyboard.

"Dad! Dad!" Ruth shouted.

Simon Gold literally jumped up from his seat.

"Are you kids crazy?" he sputtered. But seeing the frightened looks on their faces, he quickly changed his tack.

"What happened to you?" he asked, as he looked from one face to another. "Jacob, you're as white as a ghost. Are you sick? Is there something wrong? What happened?"

"Well, it's like this, Dad," Benjy began, anxious to get his side of the story in first. "Someone tried to kill me. And Jake. But we karated them good, didn't we, Jake? Pow! Wham! Kapow! Whoosh!" Benjy demonstrated.

"What Benjy means, Dad," Ruth said, pushing her brother aside. "We were having some problems with something we found and we were trying to figure it out but this guy tried something I'm not sure what and —" Ruth couldn't stop talking, even though she realized she wasn't making much sense.

"What? What are you kids talking about?" Mr. Gold was becoming more and more frustrated trying to find out what had happened.

"It's really quite simple, Dad," Izzy answered in a surprisingly cool and steady voice. He knew he had to come clean. "We — I — found a secret message in your computer. I know I wasn't supposed to be playing with it, but I wanted to show you —" Tears started to well up in his eyes. "Anyway, in trying to figure out who sent the message and what it meant, we put ourselves in real danger. Someone just tried to kill Benjy and Jake."

Simon Gold stared at his children. His mind was working at a million miles a minute.

"Now listen, all of you," he commanded. "I want you all to stay right here. Nobody moves, you understand?" They all nodded. The children had never seen their father so agitated. "I'm going to get your mother and call the police. But nobody, nobody move."

With that, Mr. Gold ran out of the room shouting his wife's name and screaming for someone to lock the door.

Chapter 6
The Inspector

By the time Inspector Shlomo Kohen of the Jerusalem Police Force arrived at number 14 Jabotinsky, Jake was feeling much better. The inspector led him through the entire encounter with the attacker, often making him repeat certain parts of his story over and over again. He was particularly interested in the intercepted message which the children gave him.

Benjy's version of the attack was much more exciting. He insisted the inspector grill him, "like in the movies," and he actually enjoyed going over the same thing a number of times. It gave him a chance to "add some important points." According to Benjy a small army of knife-wielding murderers had tried to kidnap/kill — he changed that part at least half a dozen times — him. Only the combined karate skills of himself and his big brother had saved the day. Inspector Kohen handled it all quite well, acting alternately amazed and awed at Benjy's unbelievable tale. He even asked Benjy some questions about the two "ninjas" who were the leaders of this band of crazed killers.

"Thank you, Benjy," the inspector finally concluded with a smile. Benjy was a little annoyed at being interrupted just as he was getting to "the best part," as he called it.

"I realize this must be a great strain on all of you," Inspector Kohen said, turning his attention to the rest of the family, all seated in Mr. Gold's study.

"I'm only sorry that you children didn't notify us sooner. But, at least we now have the message and our office will proceed from here. I don't believe you will have to pursue your leads any further. We'll take care of the tenants' organization and any follow-up information. And, as a matter of security, I would ask that none of you talks about this to anyone."

"Of course, Inspector," Mr. Gold began, "but what about the attack on Benjamin and Jacob? Obviously, whoever these people are they must feel my kids know too much. I don't want to sound melodramatic, but don't you think it would be a good idea for us to move out of this building for a few days, take a holiday or something?"

"Personally, Mr. Gold," the inspector responded, "I think the children's imaginations may have been playing tricks on them. Accepting, for the moment, that there was someone fighting with them, it may very well be that Benjamin interrupted a burglary in progress.

"My advice to you, Mr. Gold, is to stay right here and go about your business as usual, at least for the time being. I will, however, station a policeman in the vicinity for the next few days, just as a precaution."

Simon Gold was not convinced that the attack was just the result of a botched burglary. But there was little he could do about it at this point.

"As you wish, Inspector," he said, not wanting to express his doubts in front of the family. "We'll do as you suggest, for now."

"That's fine, Mr. Gold," the inspector assured him, as he began to get ready to leave. "Please let me know if anything further occurs, or if you remember any additional information."

The inspector left. Mrs. Gold, who had kept quiet until now, quickly bundled all the children off to bed, warding off their protests with the simple, undeniable statement, "You've all had enough excitement for one day."

When the children were in bed, although hardly asleep, she quietly entered her husband's study.

"Topper," she whispered, half in a whimper. Simon turned around. He had tried to enter some information into his computer, but his thoughts kept wandering back to what had happened.

"Yes, Naomi?" he answered softly. He walked over to her.

"Topper, I'm scared," she cried, leaning against him. He put his arms around her.

"Don't worry, darling," he said, trying to sound convincing. "It will be all right."

But he had a gut feeling that things would never be the same again.

Chapter 7
Cell Leader Demhca

Inspector Kohen left the Gold home smiling and shaking hands with everyone, trying very hard to assure them that he had things well in hand. But he was worried. He quickly decided to station not one, but two of his best men around the apartment house.

Despite what he had told Mr. Gold, the inspector was convinced that the attack had been planned, but kidnapping, not murder, was clearly the attacker's intent.

Could it be that a child was the "Primary Target" mentioned in the message? he wondered. What use would a child be to terrorists? And why pick on this particular family? And what could the "Secondary Air Target" possibly be? Surely not an Israeli aircraft? The questions seemed endless.

Sitting in his car, the inspector re-read the message. "CELL LEADER DEMHCA...COMMANDER BUKAY...HOSTAGE ONLY...STRIKE DATE: 12TH OF RAMADAN..." The Moslem month of Ramadan had already started. There were only three days left until the 12th.

But it was more than the timing. There was something about the early words of the message that sounded so familiar, as though he had seen those very same words before...but where?

Again he stared at the words. "CELL LEADER DEM-HCA...COMMANDER BUKAY...DEMHCA...BUKAY..." He knew these names. He was sure of it.

When he got back to his office it was late. Most of his men had gone home and the evening shift was hard at work. No one thought it unusual to see the inspector's light on. Behind his back most of the others referred to him respectfully as Inspector Sniffer. He was one man who never gave up on a case. Even when there were no more leads to follow, the "sniffer" would go through the files over and over again until something within him clicked, and then he'd be off checking out a newly discovered angle. Very often his hunches came to nothing; but every once in a while they paid off. For him, that made all the nights of searching worthwhile.

For his wife, Heftzi, Shlomo Kohen's devotion to his work was something less than admirable. More than once their marriage had been on the verge of collapse, but somehow Shlomo had been able to find a way to convince Heftzi to hang on just a little longer.

The inspector phoned home.

"Hi, Heftzi," he said. "Don't say a thing. Just pack our bags. We're going on that great vacation I promised you."

"What? Shlomo, is that you?" Heftzi asked, not sure

she had heard right. It had been six long years since they had gone on any vacation.

"Shlomo, are you all right? I mean, things are not so bad that I need a vacation, although God knows, it wouldn't hurt. Is there something you want to tell me? Oh, I bet I know! You had a department physical and they found something. I knew it! All those years of over-working. Oh, my God, I bet I know...oh please...don't let it be...tell me it isn't?...Is it?..." By now Heftzi had worked herself up to near hysteria. She was certain of the worst...it was only a matter of time.

Shlomo couldn't keep from laughing.

"Heftzi...Heftzi...hold on a minute. I'm fine. I have nothing to hide. Really. I just thought it would be a good idea for us to get away for a while. We certainly deserve it. I thought maybe a few days at the Kinneret. Relaxing...rowing...touring...maybe even some skiing up on Mt. Hermon?"

"Oh, Shlomo, I'm so happy I could cry. Great, we'll have the time of our lives. When are we going?"

"The day after tomorrow."

"What? But Shlomo — "

"Come on, Heftzi, let's do it before I change my mind, or the department gives me something so hot I can't leave."

Heftzi saw how much he wanted to go. But something in the back of her mind told her there was more to this than just sudden impulse.

"Okay, darling," she gladly agreed, "but just one question."

"Sure, Heftzi, what is it?"

"Is it part of a case?"

Shlomo was silent for a moment. "Well, maybe just a little part of a case," he admitted, apologetically.

"I thought so," Heftzi responded, a bit downcast, "but I'm glad to go just the same. As long as you don't spend all your time with the case."

"You can be sure I'm going to spend all my time with you. Most of it, anyway." He was glad that was over with. "I've still got some work to finish and then I'll head home. Give me another hour, okay?"

"Fine, dear. Take your time. I'll be waiting. Love you. Goodbye."

"Goodbye," Shlomo answered, and hung up. Immediately, he dialed the Gold family.

"Hello, Mr. Gold, this is Inspector Kohen. Uh...Mr. Gold, I've been giving the matter some more thought and I've decided your idea is not so bad after all."

"What idea is that?" Mr. Gold asked, suddenly feeling that his worst fears were soon to be realized.

"The idea about you and your family taking a short vacation."

"Fine, Inspector," Mr. Gold answered, worried about the sudden change of heart. "When should we go, and where?"

"For security reasons I'd rather not tell you over the phone where you're going. I'll have my men come around the day after tomorrow, bright and early, to take you and your family to some place secure and relaxing. Pack enough things for about a week."

"Pack for a week!" Mr. Gold exclaimed. "In one day? How can we pack all the kids and ourselves in just one day? Be reasonable, Inspector. After all the kids have been through today, I think we need a few days to rest. My poor wife — "

"Believe me, Mr. Gold," Inspector Kohen interrupted in a flat dry voice that made it clear he was not about to compromise, "I realize what all this entails. Truthfully, I would have preferred tomorrow morning, but I knew that would be impossible."

"What made you change your mind so fast, Inspector?" Mr. Gold asked, anxious to hear exactly how serious the situation really was.

"As you Americans like to say, 'It's better to be safe than sorry.'"

"I suppose so," said Mr. Gold, aware that he was not going to get any more out of the inspector. "I'll break the news to everyone tomorrow, but my wife is going to be fit to be tied."

"I'm really sorry, Mr. Gold. I'm sure you understand." The inspector paused for a moment on the phone. Simon didn't know whether to hang up or not. "There is one more thing I must ask of you," the inspector suddenly continued. "I would like all of you out of your apartment just for the morning. We need to check a few things in the apartment house, and I think it would be better if you all were out of the way. I'll send a young man over to give you a short tour of the Old City. Expect him around eight o'clock."

"But how are we going to get ready?" Mr. Gold began

again, feeling terribly pressured. "How can we pack?"

"Don't worry, I'm sure you'll find the time. It will only be for a few hours."

Before Simon could utter any protest, the phone went dead. Things were moving so fast. But he knew he had no choice. The inspector was a pro. In the last analysis, they would do whatever he said.

Shlomo Kohen hung up the phone as if it were a hot potato. He didn't want to argue with Mr. Gold any more, especially since he really didn't have the answers to his questions.

He looked down at the message again. It was more than a hunch that made him look for a safe house for this family. It was a matter of life and death. For, Inspector Kohen had figured out the message: CELL LEADER DEMHCA and COMMANDER BUKAY were the two most ruthless terrorists known to operate within Israel's borders. Except that he knew them as Achmed Fahr Joudey and Yakub Fousemma, part of an underground cell that had already killed three Israelis and wounded countless more.

They must have felt pretty secure, he thought, because all they did to hide their identities was to spell their names backwards. Demhca is Achmed all right, and Bukay, the notorious Yakub. How those kids were able to intercept this message I still don't understand. But, one thing is certain, these terrorists would have no qualms about killing the whole family if they felt they might spoil their plans.

But why this family? It was a question that continued

to haunt him.

He typed Simon Gold's name into his computer. Expecting to find no response, he was amazed when the computer spat back, Top Secret Confidential. He typed in the appropriate codes and was rewarded with a long list of Mr. Gold's credentials, and a brief summary of his work with MULTICOP.

"Uh-oh!" he grumbled. "That's it." Now he understood why these two top terrorists were after the Gold family. HOSTAGE ONLY the message had read. They had hoped to take Benjamin as a hostage.

His mind was racing, thinking of all the possibilities, even as he called a special number to arrange for a small squad of commandos to be dispatched to the hotel they would be staying at. By this time tomorrow the Shalom Hotel, situated on Lake Kinneret, would be a mini-fortress filled with Israeli agents.

That should make me feel better, he thought as he prepared to go home.

But it didn't.

Chapter 8

The Missing Stroller

Good morning, everyone!" Mr. Gold announced as he entered the kitchen. The family was busy eating breakfast. "Surprise for the day is that there is no school," he continued, as all eyes looked up, "and that we're going on a tour of the Old City, especially the Wailing Wall!"

"Yea!" a chorus of voices answered.

"So, hurry and finish breakfast, and let's move out!" Mr. Gold commanded in his best Wagons Ho! voice.

Naomi Gold was busy feeding Rachel, the infant, pretending that the spoon she was holding was an airplane coming in for a landing. She kept saying, "Open the hangar; here comes the plane," as she tried to swoop the spoon down into Rachel's mouth. Rachel, however, was in a playful mood, and kept squirming and moving her head so that, more often than not, the "plane" crash-landed on her cheek or chin. She found this very funny. Mrs. Gold found it frustrating.

"We'll leave Rebecca and Rachel at the baby-sitter's

house," Mr. Gold said.

"No! I want to go too!" Rebecca whined.

"Bekka, you can't go. But we'll bring you something back," Mr. Gold hoped that a bribe would end the conversation.

No such luck.

Rebecca slithered down her chair, and under the table. She sat yoga fashion, with her head down on her folded hands.

"I want to go too!" she repeated emphatically.

"Well, you can't go, Rebecca," Mr. Gold countered, talking to the table, "and that's that."

But that definitely was not that.

"Then Benjy can't go either," Rebecca insisted. "And Mommy can't go," she continued, her head unmoving.

"Look, Rebecca," said her father, crawling under the table, "be a good girl. You know you can't walk so much and we can't take the stroller where we're going, so you have to stay. But we're going to bring you something great back, and not for Benjy, just for you." Mr. Gold quickly winked at Benjy to make him understand that, of course, if Rebecca got a bribe he would get one too.

He had hoped that bribery and logic would work.

They didn't.

Rebecca now began the Israeli shoulder-raising ritual. No matter what her father said, she would no longer talk, only raise one shoulder to her ear. This was her way of saying, "I don't care what you tell me, I'm going to do what I want and not listen to you."

Simon hated the shoulder-twitching treatment. It made

him so angry that he could not reason. His only hope now was Naomi, whose resolve — and training — helped her to withstand the frustration of Rebecca's shoulder twitch.

"Naomi," Simon pleaded, as he came out from under the table, "you talk to her."

"I'm sorry, dear," Naomi answered, "this is your debate and you have to finish it."

"Debate?" Simon cried. "What debate? A debate needs two people to talk, not one talker and one twitcher!"

"Well, I think you should get back under the table and try again, dear," Naomi prompted, trying hard to conceal a smile.

"Humph!" Simon grumbled, turning back to the table. "Rebecca, please be a good girl. I'll get you a new Wizard of Oz video cassette."

A shoulder twitch was the reply.

"Or, how about a bottle for your doll?"

This time Rebecca looked up for a moment, thought about it, and then...the twitch again.

"Naomi!" Simon called out, "I think I'm losing. Maybe you could help me a little."

"I've got to change the baby and get everyone ready. You handle it." Before he could continue pleading, everyone filed out of the kitchen.

Fifteen minutes later everyone was dressed and ready in the living room. Mrs. Gold called to her husband, who was still in the kitchen with Rebecca. After a moment, he came out holding their daughter in his arms.

"How'd you do, Dad?" Jake asked. Mr. Gold twitched one shoulder, smiling. "We compromised, right, Rebecca?" Rebecca nodded her approval. "I agreed to take her, her doll and blanket with us, and she agreed to be a good girl from now on, right, Bekka?" Rebecca nodded again.

"Good going, Dad," Jake said. "Next time I ask for a new basketball I'll make sure Bekka does my negotiating for me." Everyone laughed, even Mr. Gold.

"Okay, okay, let's just get going. Inspector Kohen is sending someone to show us around." Just then, the bell rang. "Uh, perfect timing," Mr. Gold said. "Open the door, Ruth."

When Ruth opened the door, she saw a young soldier, about 18 years old, standing at attention in front of her. He had an Uzi submachine gun slung across his shoulder. He was thin, slightly tanned, and wore a leather kipah (skullcap).

"Hi, my name is Donny Steinberg," he announced in perfect English.

Ruth let him in and everyone shook hands with the young soldier.

"We're going to walk to the Kotel, the Wailing Wall, from here," he said.

"Walk?" Izzy yelped. "How can we walk? Look at Mom! She's pregnant, and Rebecca is only three, and...and..."

"And you hate to walk," Ruth prompted.

"That's beside the point," Izzy shot back. "I just think a taxi would be better...and more convenient."

"Don't worry about me, Isaac," Mrs. Gold said. "I like to walk and it's good for me. We're going to have to take the stroller anyway, thanks to your father's great bargaining powers, so there's really no problem. I think you're the only problem, dear," Mrs. Gold smiled.

"Well then, can I take a taxi?" Izzy suggested.

Mr. Gold gave his son a piercing glance. Izzy decided it was better to drop the whole thing. The group dropped Rachel at the baby-sitter's in the next apartment house. Then, they walked down Jabotinsky Street to King David Street, made a left, passing the King David Hotel. Izzy suggested they "rest" at the hotel, but everyone just ignored him.

At the bottom of King David Street, they made a right turn and walked straight to the Jaffa Gate. Donny began explaining about the Jaffa Gate and the King David Tower beyond it. The children gathered around him, but were more interested in his personal life than his history lesson.

"I thought most guys with kipahs don't join the army," Jake said.

"That's not true," Donny explained. "There are plenty of us in the army. I'm in what's called the Hesder movement."

"What's that?" Izzy asked.

"It's a five-year plan of army life and religious studies. Usually you go into the program with a bunch of your friends and alternate between learning and army until your time is up."

"Wow!" Jake whistled. "Five years is a long time, isn't it? Why don't you just do three years straight army?"

"Well, I don't want to be away from learning so long, and —"

"Hey, Donny!" Benjy interrupted, not quite clear what the discussion had been all about. "That's a neat gun," he marvelled. Donny looked down and patted Benjy's head. Benjy hated that, but if he could find out more about the gun, he would put up with it.

"How many people you kill?" Benjy asked, more to the point this time.

Ruth pushed Benjy. "Benjy, what kind of a question is that to ask? Don't you see that Donny is talking? Why don't you listen? You might learn something for a change."

"That's all right," Donny said. "Benjy, I haven't shot anyone. Believe me, I would rather not have had to fight, or kill."

Benjy, hearing his two favorite words, fight and kill began showing Donny some of his fancy kung-fu footwork.

"They ever teach you stuff like this?" he asked, kicking his feet and waving his hands in the air. "Watch this!" he commanded, kicking hard and double-punching the air in front of him.

"Very nice, Benjy," Donny responded, looking suitably impressed. "But you'd better watch out for — "

Before Donny could finish his warning, Benjy, his ego flying higher than his feet, lunged forward, failing to see the metal pole lying across the street. Kapow! He fell, scraping his elbows and knees.

"Are you all right?" Mr. Gold shouted, rushing over to help Benjy.

"Of course, yeah, sure," Benjy answered, picking himself up, obviously embarrassed. "I — I did it on purpose, to show Donny how good I fall."

"Well, you certainly fell well," Donny assured him. "Did it hurt?"

"Are you kidding?" Benjy winced, a look of pain flashing across his face. "I've lots more stuff like that to show you," he boasted, "but maybe we should keep going." He straightened himself up and, limping slightly, began to walk.

Donny led the family through the Jaffa Gate and into the shuk, the Arab marketplace that wound its way toward the Wailing Wall. There was a shorter route, through the Jewish Quarter, which Donny very much wanted to take. But everyone was anxious to see the stores and shops. And anyway, Donny reasoned, there were throngs of people and soldiers everywhere.

Donny took the lead, with the children walking behind and on either side of him. Jake wheeled the stroller with Rebecca in it. Mr. and Mrs. Gold brought up the rear.

Not far behind them lurked a husky Arab, his kafiyah covering his head and most of his face. His job was simple: to watch the Gold family and, if the opportunity presented itself, to kidnap one of the children. He had no weapons on him, just in case he was stopped and searched.

"Let's rest," Izzy pleaded, "Mom seems tired."

Mrs. Gold looked at her son. She certainly was not tired, but it was clear that he was.

"Okay, Isaac," she said, feeling sorry for him, "let's rest."

Everyone gathered at the stall of an Arab vendor sell-
ing a wide range of items, from jewelry to shoes. Seeing
such a large group of Americans, the Arab left his other
customers and rushed over to Mr. Gold.

"Shalom, shalom," he began, in a traditional Jewish
greeting. "What can I show the mister and his beautiful
family? A beautiful brass bowl perhaps," he pointed to his
brass selection, "or, a beautiful emerald dagger of the
16th century?" He displayed his dagger and sword collection. Benjy's eyes fairly popped out of his head with desire. "Or perhaps a beautiful jade neck — "

"Thank you very much," Mr. Gold interrupted, "but
what we would really like is a beautiful rest before we buy
anything."

The vendor saw Mrs. Gold's condition and immediately
brought out a chair for her to rest on. Izzy eyed the chair
longingly, but before he could say a word, the Arab
brought him a chair, too.

"Uh, Dad, why don't you sit down next to Mom," Izzy
said, half-heartedly.

"No thanks, Izzy, you sit down. I want to look at the
merchandise."

Mr. Gold started looking around the stall. Donny stood
guard in front. The children, except for Izzy, began looking through the goods too.

The Arab trailing them pretended to be interested in
some sheep hides hanging from a nearby stall. "Hey," Mr.
Gold said, coming upon a mound of hats. "What about
some hats?"

"Great," Ruth answered as she began to pick through

the hats. She began trying on one hat after another. Izzy finally got up and went to the hats too. Benjy joined in, biding his time until he could talk about what he really wanted. Jake left Rebecca asleep in the stroller near his mother and went to look through the hats as well.

Pretty soon hats were flying everywhere. Mr. Gold had the biggest problem. No hat seemed to fit him except an extra-large, red, short-brimmed one that had "Shriner's Convention 1981" written on it in big black letters. Ruth and Jake took matching "I Love Israel" hats with a zipper compartment on the side. Izzy chose a tan hat which had a picture of a lone goose flying into the sunset. Even Mrs. Gold got up to join in the fun. She chose a plain all-white hat. Only Benjy was being difficult.

"Which one do you want, Benjamin?" Mrs. Gold asked.

"I don't know," he answered gloomily.

"Come on, Benjamin, surely you want one of these beautiful hats," Mrs. Gold prompted, holding up an assortment for him to choose from.

"Nah, I don't think so." Benjy left very little doubt that he was upset about something.

"Okay," his mother said, putting down the hats and lifting his face, "what's the problem, dear?"

Everyone was looking at Benjy. Even Donny had turned around, curious as to what was troubling his favorite nudnik. No one even noticed as an Arab swiftly and quietly moved toward the stroller just outside the stall.

"I want the knife," Benjy finally announced.

"What knife?" his father asked.

"The one with the diamonds and rubies and stuff."

"But you can't carry a knife around," Mr. Gold told him.

"I'm not gonna carry it. I'm gonna protect everyone with it. You think I don't know knife fighting? Well, I do." Benjy began slashing an imaginary foe.

"Simon," Mrs. Gold called to her husband, "I think we had better choose our hats and start going. Benjy is just going to have to live with the fact that he cannot have a knife."

Benjy had tears in his eyes.

The Arab reached the stroller and began moving it, with its occupant, down the cobbled street. He was half pushing, half carrying the lightweight stroller, smiling to himself at how easy it had been.

"Wait, mister," the vendor shouted, afraid of losing a deal. "I have another beautiful knife here."

"I think we've had enough knives," Mr. Gold angrily answered him. "Please don't make the situation worse than it is."

"No, mister, you do not understand," the vendor continued, anxious to make his point. "This is a special, beautiful knife for your beautiful son."

As he spoke, the vendor pulled out a long knife. Donny, seeing the knife, cocked and raised his Uzi in one swift motion, pointing the gun barrel directly at the vendor's head.

"Aiiii!" the vendor screamed, quickly dropping the knife. "See! See!" he pointed. "See! It is a no real knife!"

Sure enough, it was a rubber knife painted silver. Absolutely harmless. Benjy picked it up and smiled. Donny uncocked his Uzi, and everyone breathed a deep sigh of relief.

*Donny, seeing the knife, cocked and raised his Uzi in one
swift motion, pointing the gun barrel directly
at the vendor's head.*

Meanwhile, the kidnapper was at the bottom of the street. He turned into an alley and came to a locked door. Quietly he knocked twice, waited, and then knocked three times more.

"Mahmud," a voice inside said.

"Yakub," the man outside answered.

The door clicked wide open. The man and the stroller were swallowed up inside.

"I simply must sit down," Mrs. Gold said, obviously still tense from what had happened. "This a little too much excitement for someone in my condition." Everyone laughed, more to relieve the tension than anything else.

The vendor was also a little shaky from his near fatal experience. Benjy, however, was cradling the knife, lovingly.

"How much for all the hats...and the knife?" Mr. Gold looked at his son and knew the knife was sold.

"One hundred and fifty shekels," the vendor answered, straight-faced. He felt certain that he would get a little of his aggravation back, in money.

"Fine," Mr. Gold said, realizing he was being had, but embarrassed by the whole situation. He felt the Arab had suffered a great deal. If money would make him feel better, then he would pay.

He took out his wallet and began counting the money.

"No good, Dad," Izzy suddenly declared.

"What?" his father asked, staring at his son.

"That's a rip-off, Dad. Let me handle it."

Mr. Gold stood there, amazed at Isaac's sudden self-confidence. The boy had always had a head for business, but he had never bargained for anything before, at least not to Mr. Gold's knowledge.

"We'll give you 80 shekels for the lot," Izzy announced to the astonished vendor.

"Wait a second, Iz — " Mr. Gold began, but Izzy politely cut him off. "Please, Dad, let me handle this." Then, turning back to the vendor, "80 shekels or we walk."

"For such beautiful hats, for such a beautiful knife? Please, mister, I am losing money at 150 shekels."

The vendor spoke directly to Mr. Gold, hoping that he would stick up for him.

"I'm sorry," Mr. Gold apologized, feeling sorry for the man, "but as of now my son does all my bargaining," he asserted with pride.

"No!" the vendor firmly declared, prepared to do battle. "One hundred and twenty-five shekels, but that is my last price offer for these beautiful things."

"Yeah, well, 90 beautiful shekels is mine." With that, Izzy took his father's hand and started to walk out of the stall.

"Hey!" yelled Benjy. "Are you crazy? What about my knife? Dad, Mom, talk to him. He's gone crazy! You can't let him do this!" Benjy kept protesting, even as everyone prepared to leave.

The vendor realized that Izzy meant business, but he could not let himself be outdone by a child.

"Wait!" he shouted. "You are such nice people, beautiful people, with beautiful mother going to have beautiful baby. I give you present. Only 100 shekels for everything."

"Well..." Izzy looked at the vendor for a moment, wondering if he dared press his luck any further. "Well..." he said again, watching everyone hang on his words.

"Well, you better say yes or I'm gonna kill you with this knife!" Benjy held up the rubber knife and looked as if he meant it.

"It's a deal!" Izzy smiled, shaking the vendor's hand.

Everyone started to clap, even Donny. Only Benjy was angry for having been put through such a terrible ordeal.

"Oh my God! Simon!" Mrs. Gold suddenly shouted. "Who's got the stroller? The stroller with Rebecca in it?"

Everyone ran to Mrs. Gold. Ruth started looking around for the stroller, but it was obvious the stroller was gone. Donny shouted "Stay where you are," and ran out of the stall and down the cobbled steps. As he ran, his eyes were constantly scanning each stall, looking for the stroller. Some soldiers saw him running and offered to help. They spread out and began asking passers-by if they had seen anyone with a stroller, anyone suspicious.

Finally, an elderly couple said they had seen an Arab with a stroller making a right turn at the bottom of the steps. Donny, followed by a group of soldiers, gave chase.

Meanwhile, back at the vendor's stall, Mrs. Gold had fainted. Her husband didn't know what to do. In his broken Hebrew, he asked some passing soldiers to get help.

Ruth, unable to keep still, began looking through the other stalls. She realized the search was hopeless but she felt she had to do something. Tears welled up in her eyes as she ran from stall to stall.

Jake and Izzy, seeing their sister searching the stalls, warned her not to go too far. But by now she was out of control. She began running in and out of stalls. Vendors started yelling at her but she paid no attention to them. Each time she saw a stroller, she ran over to it, but each stroller and its occupant belonged to someone else.

Ruth had worked herself up into a frenzy. She was crying and yelling, "Bekka! Bekka!" Jake, preoccupied with his mother, told Izzy to get Ruth. He ran to her but she pushed him away, shouting, "Leave me alone! I've got to find Bekka!" Izzy was afraid of her in this state. He didn't know how to handle her. With every second, Ruth was getting wilder and wilder, shouting Rebecca's name at the top of her lungs.

Donny ran down the steps, taking them two and three at a time. At the bottom he turned right. He started walking now, more careful not to miss anything, his gun at the ready. Then he saw it about five yards away. The stroller, turned on its side. He ran to it. Lying nearby was Rebecca's doll. But Rebecca was nowhere to be seen.

Donny picked up the stroller and stuffed the doll inside it. All the stalls nearby were locked. When the other soldiers caught up with him, he told them to check every stall in the vicinity, even if it meant breaking down the doors. Then he began the sad walk back to the Gold family.

Ruth was hysterical. She was circling the same stalls over and over again. People were looking at her as if she were crazy. Even the soldiers began shouting at her to calm down.

Finally, more from exhaustion than anything else, Ruth sat down on the floor and, burying her head in her hands, began to sob. At that moment, she just wanted to die.

So, naturally, she barely felt the little fingers that touched her shoulder. Hardly heard the small voice that said, "Don't cry, Ruthy, we'll find my doll. Don't cry."

Ruth was almost afraid to look up. When she did, she saw her. Rebecca. She jumped up and shouted, "Rebecca! Look, everyone, it's Rebecca!"

Jake and Izzy stopped in their tracks. They could hardly believe their eyes. There was Rebecca, comforting Ruth! Ruth picked Rebecca up and brought her back to the family. Mrs. Gold, who had by now regained consciousness, grabbed Rebecca and hugged her, crying all the while. Jake and Izzy also began crying for joy. Even Benjy had tears in his eyes. Everyone hugged one another, happy and delirious with having found Rebecca safe.

Donny, trudging up the street with the stroller, saw the family crying and hugging each other and assumed they were comforting each other over their loss. With downcast face he went to explain to the family how he had failed, miserably, in his mission to protect them. For Donny, this was not just a failed mission; this was a disaster for which he knew he would pay the rest of his life.

By the time he reached the family, Donny too had tears in his eyes. Rebecca, seeing him holding the stroller, jumped out of her mother's arms and ran over to Donny.

"You found it! You found my dolly!" she screamed for

joy. Quick as a whip, she grabbed the doll from his hands. "But look, it has a hole in it," she cried, showing Donny a big hole in the doll's chest.

Donny didn't hear a word she said. He was stunned. All he could think of was that Rebecca was alive. Alive!

Before she knew what had happened, Donny grabbed her, picked her up and hugged her hard.

"Ouch!" she protested. "You're hurtin' me." He let her down and she ran back to her waiting mother.

Donny and the family quickly exchanged stories and then all eyes fixed on Rebecca.

"Where were you?" Ruth scolded.

"I went to get milk for my baby," Rebecca proudly answered, showing the filled milk bottle she had been holding in her hands the whole time.

"But where did you get the milk?" Donny asked.

"From the milkman, silly," she answered, wondering how come grownups didn't know such things. And then she pointed to a stall where an Arab vendor waved to her. "He gave me milk for my baby."

Everyone went over to the Arab to thank him. He was a little taken aback, by all these well-wishers. But, after Mr. Gold bought everything in sight — without Isaac bargaining — the man was very content to let these "crazy Americans" have their way.

"I think we should go back now," Donny said, as soon as things had gotten back to order.

"Oh, no," Mrs. Gold answered. "Now, more than ever, we should give thanks at the Wailing Wall."

What can I say to that? Donny thought to himself,

proud of the strength of this unusual family.

"All right," he said out loud, "but we don't stop for anything."

They all readily agreed.

Yakub was seething. His men had had a good laugh at his expense, each threatening to kill his doll.

Finally, in a fit of rage, he grabbed the doll, stuck his knife in it, and tossed it, and the stroller, out the door.

He knew the Israelis would find the stroller. But by then he and his men would be long gone.

"Let it be a warning," he said to his men. "Next time we shall not fail!"

Chapter 9
The Collector

The Gold family walked down the cobblestones of the shuk toward the Wailing Wall. None of the children had ever seen the Wall — the Kotel — before. They had heard stories about this famous wall of the Second Temple Period. For them, as for many Jews, this fortress was a symbol of another time, a time when the Holy Temple had been the center of every Jew's life.

So, when they rounded the last vendor's stall and headed for the steps leading down to the Kotel, the kids were filled with anticipation, hardly able to contain themselves.

Suddenly, 2,000 years of Jewish history loomed up in front of them. Almost as one, they stopped and stared. "Gee!" Izzy whispered. "That's some Wall!"

"It sure is," said Ruth. "I'll go with Mom and Bekky to the women's side. I'll meet you guys later." They walked toward the Wall, acutely aware of the holiness that filled this place. The boys also began walking, their eyes surveying the giant stones.

"Well, what do you think of it?" Mr. Gold asked, as they got within arm's length of the Wall.

"It's great, Dad," Jake answered, unable to take his eyes off it.

"I can't believe we're actually here," Izzy said, in a tone of awe.

"I thought it was going to be a lot bigger," complained Benjy. "At least up to the sky."

Mr. Gold laughed. "Don't worry, Benjy, the prayers people say here reach the sky."

"How?" Benjy asked, taking his father's words literally.

"Well, I'll tell you what my father, may he rest in peace, told me the first time I saw the Kotel and asked him the same question."

The other children turned their attention to their father, sensing that what he was going to say would interest them too.

Groups of men on either side of them were lost in prayer. In one corner, dozens of chanting men were holding a young boy aloft, obviously celebrating his bar mitzvah. Mr. Gold spoke in a low voice, careful not to disturb the groups praying or those nearby singing.

"Look up there," he pointed about halfway up the Wall. "See, there's a bird quietly watching everyone."

The children all looked up and saw the bird.

"Hey," Jake said, "that's only a gray pigeon."

"Yes," Mr. Gold agreed, "it's a gray pigeon. But the word 'only' does not apply. Look around. Notice that there are no other pigeons here, only lots and lots of sparrows, all flitting around. They go back and forth, over our heads. Now, watch carefully."

In a few moments, the pigeon opened its wings and began to soar, slowly, solemnly, in sharp contrast to the staccato flight of the other birds. After a few seconds, the pigeon once again came to rest on its perch.

"You're right, Dad," Izzy said. "There's only that one pigeon. But he doesn't seem interested in going anywhere in particular."

"Oh, but that's where you're wrong, Isaac," his father gently said. "That pigeon," Mr. Gold pointed again, "is called the Collector."

"The Collector?" Benjy echoed. "What's he collecting? Worms?"

"No, Benjy, not worms. Prayers."

"Oh come on, Dad," Jake said sarcastically, "how is a bird going to collect prayers? Birds don't even know what prayers are."

"I'm not so sure of that, Jacob. We believe that all living things pray, in their own way, to God. But, in any event, as my father explained it, since the destruction of our Second Temple almost 2,000 years ago, there has always been a Collector bird at the Kotel."

"But what does the bird do when he's collected the prayers?" asked Izzy.

"Good question, Isaac. Each night, at exactly midnight, the Collector bird flies up, up and away. No one knows exactly where, but he's not seen any more until the first rays of the morning sun. Stranger still, when he returns, his gray color has changed to pure white."

Everyone was quiet for a moment. Thinking.

"But I still want to know what the bird does with the prayers," persisted Izzy.

"Well, there are those who say that the angel Gabriel meets the Collector and draws the prayers from him. Even the tears of those who have prayed at the Kotel are collected by the bird. These tears are also weighed to determine whose prayers are to be answered at once, whose later on, and whose not at all. As the prayers are drawn from the Collector, his gray color changes to white. When he has transferred all the prayers, the bird flies back to the Kotel."

"You mean sometimes a person's prayers are not answered?" Benjy naively asked.

"Certainly, Benjamin," his father explained. "Sometimes it is better for the person not to have his prayers answered. God knows what is good for you even if you don't. Understand?"

"Nope," Benjy answered honestly.

"Well, look at it this way," his father tried rewording his explanation to suit a six-year-old. "Supposing you come to the Wall and pray for...for..." Mr. Gold thought for a moment and then a smile spread across his face. "Suppose you prayed real hard for a Karate Kid Hand Stomper. That's what you decided you wanted more than anything else in the world."

"Aw, Dad," Benjy was stunned, and a little embarrassed. He couldn't imagine how his father knew he wanted the Stomper. After all, except for his mother, he had told no one.

"...since the destruction of our Second Temple almost 2,000 years ago, there has always been a Collector bird at the Kotel."

"Really, I wasn't going to ask for that," he lied.

"I know, Benjy. But just suppose that was your favorite thing and that's what you wanted. And suppose, after you prayed for it, God gave it to you. You would be happy, wouldn't you?"

"You bet!" Benjy heartily agreed.

"But suppose because of that Karate Kid Hand Stomper someone in the family was hurt. Wouldn't you feel terrible?"

"Who did it hurt?" Benjy asked innocently.

" Does it make a difference?" Mr. Gold answered impatiently, barely able to contain his frustration.

"Sure it does," Benjy insisted.

"Okay, suppose it hurt your little sister."

"Which one?"

"Benjamin!" his father whispered between clenched teeth.

"Oh, well, then of course I'd feel terrible," Benjy quickly answered, realizing his father was in no mood to play games. "But if it was Izzy — "

Izzy swung at Benjy's head. Benjy ducked and ran behind his father.

"Forget it, Isaac," Mr. Gold commanded, "he's only teasing you."

Benjy, seeing it was safe, came out from behind his father. Izzy quickly pinched his brother, hard, before his father could say anything.

"Ouch!" Benjy yelped.

"We're almost even, Fooey," Izzy teased.

"Stop it, both of you," Mr. Gold warned. "Now let me

finish. The point I'm trying to make is that it would have been better if God had not answered your prayers Benjy. Not answering your prayers was really what you wanted, only you didn't know it. Fortunately, God did. Get it now?"

"Yeah," Benjy pretended to understand.

Mr. Gold turned his attention back to the rest of the children.

"Anyway, to get back to what I was saying. The Collector bird is called the Maylitz in Hebrew. The people of Jerusalem, especially the old-timers, have a very high regard for him."

"But what about the other birds, those sparrow-looking ones that fly around so fast?" Izzy asked.

"Ah, yes. Those birds are the Maylitz's helpers. They scurry around, over everyone's head, plucking the prayers from the air and chirping them out to the Collector. Notice too," Mr. Gold pointed to a number of darting birds, "how they only seem to fly over the heads of people who are talking or who have just finished praying."

"Why's that, Dad?" Jake asked.

"Because it's their job to collect every word we say and transfer those words, verbatim, exactly to the Maylitz. That means that everything we say may reach the angel Gabriel. So, when we're near the Kotel we have to be careful about what we say."

"Uh-oh!" Benjy suddenly murmured.

"What's the matter now, Benjy?" his father asked, ready for more frustration.

"Uh, nothing, Dad. But Izzy, I'm sorry I teased you. I mean I'm really sorry I teased you!" Benjy shouted, watching the birds above him as he was yelling.

"Hey, Benj!" Izzy shouted back. "I can hear you, you don't have to shout."

"Yeah, well I don't care if you can hear me," Benjy whispered, pointing to the sky, "I want to make sure those bird helpers can hear me."

"Don't worry," his father assured him, "as long as you meant what you said about being sorry, the birds will hear you and relay the message."

"Uh-oh!" Benjy moaned, under his breath.

"Anyway," Mr. Gold concluded, "that's the story about the Maylitz."

Benjy suddenly shot his arm straight up into the air.

"What is it, Benjy?" his father asked. "And please don't raise your hand. This isn't school."

"Sorry," Benjy answered a little sheepishly, "I just didn't want the birds to think I was interrupting you."

"Fine, Benjy, now what is your question?"

"Well, if the birds are all carrying our prayers, why does everyone put these little pieces of paper into the Wall?" Benjy held up his own note. Each child had written a note to leave in the cracks of the Kotel.

"Let's see," Mr. Gold began groping for the right answer. An answer that Benjy would understand.

"Benjy, when you pray, your thoughts and words exist for a short moment and then are gone. You finish your prayers and go about your business. Most of the time you don't even remember what you said.

"But, when you write your prayers on a piece of paper, you actually do something to make your prayers come alive. You know the words are there, inside the cracks of the Wall, constantly asking God for whatever it is you want."

"I can understand that, Dad," Jake quickly cut in, before Benjy could ask his next question. "But what happens to the thousands and thousands of papers that people stick into the Wall? Don't tell me the birds collect them, too?"

"No, Jacob, the birds don't collect them. The way my father explained it to me was that once your prayers are collected, they become part of the Wall. That's why no matter how many pieces of paper are stuck into each crack or crevice, there's always room for more."

Just then they heard Donny calling them. He had stood back a way where he could guard both the men and the women. He waved for everyone to join him. It was getting late, and he was nervous.

Mr. Gold motioned to Donny to wait a few minutes. He and the boys then joined a group of men praying. At the conclusion of the service they headed back to Donny and the women.

"We're going back through the Jewish Quarter," Donny ordered. No one argued.

The way home was uneventful. Everyone was lost in his own thoughts, even Benjy. The boys were thinking about the story their father had told them, and about the private prayers each had tucked away into the stones of the Kotel. Simon and Naomi Gold were thinking of how fortunate they were to be in this wonderful land, where Jewish history lay like an open book for all to read. Only

Donny's thoughts were filled with the possible dangers that awaited this unsuspecting family.

"Tomorrow, I will pick you all up at 7 a.m. sharp. Please be ready," Donny said as he settled the Golds into their apartment. "It will be a long journey, so I advise you all to go right to sleep," he concluded, opening the front door.

"Hold it one minute," Mr. Gold called. "Donny, I just remembered I forgot to buy something for the trip. Can you walk me to the hotel down the block?"

"Sure, Mr. Gold," Donny said.

"Okay, I want everyone asleep by the time I come back. Ruth and Jake, put the little ones to sleep. Darling," he turned to his wife, "the older kids will take care of everything. You just turn in."

"But please don't take too long, Simon," his wife said, still nervous from the day's events.

"I'll be back in 20 minutes," he assured her.

Mr. Gold and Donny left for the hotel. Once there, Mr. Gold went straight to the store he was looking for. It was just about to close. He convinced the manager to let him in to buy one special item. Simon handed the store owner 15 shekels and took the last Karate Kid Hand Stomper off the shelf.

At least, he thought, someone's prayers will have definitely been answered.

Chapter 10
Karate Kid Hand Stomper

The next morning, the Gold family apartment looked like the site of a terrorist attack. It was only 6 a.m., but everything was in chaos. Clothes were strewn about, and children were shouting. Mr. Gold was trying, unsuccessfully, to close an overstuffed suitcase. His wife was trying, just as unsuccessfully, to find a pair of matching socks for Jacob. Little Rachel, the one-year-old, was busy watching her cereal drip onto the floor. Benjy was screaming about someone stealing the Karate Kid Hand Stomper his father had surprised him with only last night. He made sure everyone knew that without his Stomper he wasn't going on any trip, "No way."

"Quiet down, all of you," shouted Mr. Gold, as he strained to close the suitcase. "Ruth, come over here and sit on the other side of this suitcase so I can close it." Ruth didn't like feeling she was the only one heavy enough to flatten out the suitcase. She hesitated, but realized that now was not the time to make an issue of it.

"Come on, Ruth, you'll find your sneakers or whatever it is you're looking for later. Just sit down on the other end like a good girl. Good. Now, hold it, hold it down...that's it...I've almost got it...almost...almost...!"

"Wait!" Benjy screamed at the top of his lungs. The scream was so loud and intense that everyone dropped what they were doing to see if Benjy was in some sort of trouble.

"What, what's the matter?" Mr. Gold jumped up, genuinely concerned. Immediately, the latch of the suitcase popped open.

"My Karate Kid Hand Stomper!" Benjy exclaimed, as he ran to the suitcase.

"We'll look for everything later!" his father shouted back. He was really upset at having to close the suitcase again.

"No, you don't understand," Benjy continued. "My Karate Kid Hand Stomper. You're breaking it. Let me get it out!" Benjy pulled at the partially closed suitcase and took out a pint-sized doll of his hero, The Karate Kid. One of the hands of the doll had obviously been squashed when Mr. Gold tried to close the suitcase.

"You stomped my Karate Kid Hand Stomper!" Benjy wailed. "Look at him, you busted his good arm. His hitting arm. Now, how's he going to stomp anyone, huh? Tell me, how's he going to stomp 'em?" he implored, tears streaming down his face.

Simon Gold, knowing that three more suitcases, exactly like this one, filled to overflowing, still waited for him to force them closed, finally reached his breaking point.

"You stomped my Karate Kid Hand Stomper!" Benjy wailed.

"You want to see stomping?" he exploded. "That's what you want? Stomping? I'll show you stomping, right now!" Without saying another word, he turned menacingly to Benjy, one hand held high.

Benjy wisely decided it would be better for him to be in a different place, any place but in front of his father. He ran. Mr. Gold, ready to pounce, was not far behind. Mrs. Gold, fearing for her son's life and her husband's heart, also gave chase. Ruth and Izzy, afraid that their mother might give birth at any second, ran to calm her down. Rebecca began clapping madly and singing, "I had a little dreidel," while she watched the parade of runners. Little Rachel had finally reached the telephone someone had graciously left near her high chair. She was saying "baba" to the long-distance operator she had somehow managed to dial.

This was the scene that greeted Donny, who, after getting no response to his desperate knocking, broke down the door, Uzi cocked, ready to do battle to the finish.

"Mah koreh po!" (What's happening here!) Donny shouted, forgetting his English. At the sight of his gun held high, everyone in the room froze.

Rebecca, who was now singing, "Follow the yellow brick road," part of her standard repertoire, broke off her song, ran over to Donny and calmly asked, "Where's my pacifier?"

This was too much. Donny started to laugh. Before long, everyone else was laughing too. Everyone except the long-distance operator who was yelling so loudly you could hear her clear across the room. She kept asking the baby if it was an emergency call, to which the baby gave the spirited reply of either "baba," or "pee-pee," whichever came to mind.

Once the laughter began, it was hard to stop. For a full two minutes, everyone was in stitches. Mr. Gold was laughing so hard he had tears in his eyes. Benjy, seeing that the immediate danger was over, also tried a tentative smile. Donny and the children kept laughing, as Rebecca, seeing that she wasn't going to get her pacifier, began another song from her favorite video, The Wizard of Oz. Rachel abruptly threw the telephone to the floor, and started clapping. This started another peal of laughter rippling through the ranks.

By now, two undercover policemen had appeared on the scene. They were undecided as to what to do with all these laughing maniacs. Donny composed himself long enough to tell the family that they had little under an hour to get ready. That sobered everyone up, and they went back to their packing.

By 7:30 a.m., the Gold family was packed, and headed downstairs to the garage. Tying most of their luggage to the car rack, they piled into their eight-seater Peugeot 505 station wagon. With the police escort to lead them, they began the three-and-a-half-hour journey to Lake Kinneret and the Shalom Hotel.

No one paid attention to the beat-up Toyota trailing well behind them. It had been stolen just for this mission. The tinted windshield of the car hid the faces of the three terrorists inside. Their mission was to follow the Gold family to its destination, and then report back to their leader.

Chapter 11
Terrorists Attack

The trip to the Kinneret proved fairly uneventful, with only four stops for bathroom call, and two for food. This was actually a sort of record for the Gold family. But the security men had warned Simon in advance that each stop was a potential danger for the family. So he sharply curtailed their emergencies.

At their last stop, Donny had informed Mr. Gold that his men were getting edgy and that with only 45 minutes to the hotel, they would have to drive straight through, without any additional stops. When Donny returned to his car, he looked up the road and saw the same car he felt sure had been following them for some time. Its hood was raised, as though it had broken down.

"This is suspicious," he told his men. "If their car was really in trouble, they would have pulled into this service station." He went inside the station to telephone headquarters.

The terrorists were none too happy with the situation

either. With no way of knowing beforehand when the Golds would rest, they were forced to come to a screeching halt at each roadside stop. There was little cover on the road, and the only thing they could do was pretend that their car had broken down. Twice, they had to chase well-meaning motorists away, so as not to attract too much attention. But it was clear, from the way the security men were looking their way, that they had been spotted.

When the others left, the terrorists drove into the gas station. One of them called their leader and reported the situation. By now they were fairly certain that the Golds were headed for the Kinneret and to one of the small hotels that dotted the water's shoreline. They were told to wait at the station for further orders. Under no circumstances were they to follow the Golds.

Donny looked back through his rear-view mirror. Two men were pushing the Toyota into the station. Good, he thought. Maybe it had only been a false alarm. Just to be sure, he had telephoned for an extra car to meet them at the Galilee interchange to stop the Toyota if it followed them.

Donny breathed a sigh of relief, knowing the situation was stable again.

By the time everyone arrived at the Shalom Hotel, found their bungalows, unpacked, and got ready for lunch...lunch was over.

"Dad, I'm hungry," Jake said, as they gathered in the main hotel lobby.

"I'm starved," Benjy chimed in.

"Now look, gang," Ruth broke in, "Dad tried to get us

here on time. It's not his fault we're starving. I'm sure supper is soon."

"At seven!" exclaimed Izzy, looking at the bulletin board. He was almost in tears. "By then we'll all have died of hunger. Oh no, I hate this place! I want to go home! This place is — "

"Crummy!" Benjy shouted. "But I've got a great idea, gang. Let's go on a hunger strike until we get food."

"What kind of dumb thing is that to do?" questioned Izzy.

"I saw it on TV. Everyone in the prison went on a hunger strike until the head of the prison gave them what they wanted. We can do the same thing."

"But Benjy," Ruth tried to reason with him, "if we're already hungry and asking for food, how can we have a hunger strike? A hunger strike means you refuse to eat."

"So what?" Benjy insisted, trying not to look foolish. "We can still have a hunger strike after supper."

"I've got a better idea," Mrs. Gold cut in, before things got out of hand. "Why don't we ask Donny if one of his soldiers would mind getting us some food in town, wherever town is."

"That's a good idea too," Benjy assured her.

Mr. Gold was the unanimous choice to ask Donny to get food, even though he voted against it.

"Sure, Mr. Gold, we'll be delighted," Donny told Simon after he had explained their dilemma. "The inspector said you were to have whatever you wanted."

Donny sent someone, pad and pencil in hand, to take the children's orders.

"Shalom, everybody," announced a young police officer. "My name is Rivka."

"Wow!" exclaimed Benjy. "A girl policeman! Do you catch only girl robbers?"

"No, motik, in this country, men and women policemen catch both men and women criminals." Rivka had never met anyone like Benjy.

"Boy, then you must know plenty of karate, huh? I mean to catch the men criminals. Pow! Wham! Kapow!" Benjy showed her some of his fancy footwork, careful not to fall this time. "Jake, Ruth, Izzy and me all know karate great. We even beat up a whole bunch of bad guys the other day. Boy, did we stomp 'em, eh, Jake?"

Jake preferred not to answer. He was more interested in trying to decide what he wanted to eat.

"Well, I'm sure that's wonderful," Rivka answered, not exactly sure what Benjy was talking about. "We do take karate, er, what's your name?"

"Benjamin," Benjy stated.

"Yes, Benjamin, what — "

"But some people call me Benjy," he interrupted.

"Wonderful, Benjy, now what — "

"My brothers and sisters even call me Kung-fooey, but I don't like that too much," he continued, oblivious to her attempts at talking.

"Fine, Benjy," Rivka was starting to show just the slightest trace of annoyance, "but we really have to — "

"When I grow up and get called to the Torah for my bar mitzvah, then they'll call me Benjamin Shmuel, like my grandfather, Benjamin Shmuel, whom everyone called

Benjamin, like me. I don't think anyone ever called him Benjy, although my Mom says — "

Mr. Gold had overheard enough of the conversation to know that Benjy was dangerously close to finding out exactly how much karate Rivka Shamgar really knew.

"Benjamin," he called out, "unless you want to be called 'the boy with the red tushie,' you had better let Ms. Shamgar take your orders."

Benjy/Benjamin/Kung-fooey/Benjamin Shmuel blushed. Everyone else laughed.

"Sorry, Ms. Shamgar," Mr. Gold said, "but I think you can safely continue now."

Rivka wrote down all the orders and started walking out to the parking lot where her car was parked. Ruth suddenly ran over to her and shyly asked, "Rivka, can I come with you in the police car?"

Rivka smiled and said, "Sure, motik, come on."

The boys were dying to go too, but too shy to ask. They meekly followed Ruth and Rivka out the door.

The police car was at the other end of the parking lot. The two girls were having an animated conversation, walking briskly toward Rivka's vehicle. Suddenly, two big men sprang out of a parked car behind them. One grabbed Ruth and tried to force her into the car. The other, an ugly-looking man with a long scar down his right cheek, attacked the policewoman. Each girl began struggling with her captor. Rivka tried desperately to reach her gun but before she knew it she was pinned to the floor.

More by instinct than training, Ruth stomped down hard on her assailant's foot. He shouted and began cursing in Arabic, but he let go of her for a moment. Ruth, now free to use her hands, slammed her elbow viciously into her assailant's stomach. Then she bent forward, found his hurt foot and yanked it out from under him. Down he went, but not until he had grabbed her hair and forced her back down on top of him. She yelled in pain. Still holding her hair, the man pushed Ruth off him and began pulling her into the car. She let out a terrified scream.

Ruth's scream broke the trance that had held her brothers frozen in their tracks. Instantly, the boys raced to help their sister.

Hearing Ruth's scream, Rivka also seemed to find new strength. She reached over her shoulder and poked her assailant in the eye with her thumb. He let go of her as she reached for her gun. But it had fallen in the scuffle. Her attacker, recovering, grabbed Rivka and punched her in the stomach. She went down.

At that precise moment, Jake and Izzy, with Benjy shouting in the background, attacked.

Jake threw himself bodily at Ruth's attacker, catching him off-balance and shoving him, with a loud thud, against the hood of his car. He roared and grabbed Jake by the throat. Try as he could, Jake couldn't release the hold around his neck. The attacker began to squeeze until Jake, caught in a vise-like grip, started turning blue.

Izzy was struggling with Rivka's assailant when he saw his brother go limp from the stranglehold. He immediately disengaged, and ran to help Jake.

With a mighty leap, Izzy jumped onto the hood of the terrorists' car, grabbed the man's arm from behind and pulled back and up with all his might. At the same time he smashed his fist again and again in the attacker's throat. With a painful wail, the Arab released his grip on Jake, who crumpled to the ground, desperately trying to catch his breath.

Soldiers and policemen started streaming into the parking lot. The Arab who had attacked Rivka grabbed his partner and shoved him into the car. With a screeching roar, the engine ignited. Benjy decided this was the moment to leap into action. He bent down, took off one shoe and threw it with all his might at the driver of the car. Miraculously, it caught him just above the eye. Blood spurted out as a large gash appeared. The terrorist looked at Benjy with absolute hatred. This was too much for our hero. He decided he might have bitten off more than he could chew. Turning around, he hobbled as fast as he could toward the onrushing policemen.

Jake was just coming back to his senses when the roar of the engine warned him of the speeding car's approach. He quickly rolled to his left as the wheels of the car missed his head by inches. The car sped away, down the driveway and, without slowing, shot onto the road.

"Wa...Watch out!" shouted Heftzi as the terrorists' car side-swiped them. Inspector Kohen turned his wheel savagely, forcing his car off the road. They came to a grinding halt in a small ditch.

"Are you all right?" Shlomo asked his wife.

"Yes, I think so. Did you see that? What happened?" Heftzi watched the Fiat zoom away.

"I don't know, but I get the feeling we've arrived too

Inspector Kohen turned his wheel savagely, forcing his car off the road. They came to a grinding halt in a small ditch.

late to help. Did you see the blood on the driver's face? Something's happened at the hotel, that's for sure. Let me see if I can get the car started again, and back out."

Inspector Kohen tried to start his car several times, but to no avail. Finally, he and Heftzi got out, locked up, and began trudging up the long driveway of the hotel. Before long, they were met by several policemen who had given chase on foot. They stopped when they saw the inspector and immediately began filling him in on all the details of what had happened.

When the inspector and Heftzi finally reached the hotel, they saw the havoc that had been caused by the terrorists. Rivka was sitting in the parking lot, another policewoman gently comforting her. Her mouth was bloodied, and she was shaken. There was a medic taking care of her bruises. Jake was being carried to the medic by a policeman, despite his continuous protests to be put down. The finger marks of the terrorist were outlined on his neck and one eye was slightly swollen. Izzy was also being carried, but he didn't seem to mind one bit. He had a badly scraped elbow, and what seemed to be a sprained thumb.

Mr. and Mrs. Gold were hovering over Ruth who seemed dazed. But, except for the pain she still felt from having had her hair yanked, she seemed okay.

Only Benjy, who had not a single scratch on him, was complaining.

"Oh, my achin' stomach," he moaned, "my achin' head, my achin' foot," he groaned, trying to get some sympathy. Finally, Mrs. Gold, after assuring herself that Ruth was all right, went over to Benjy.

"Are you all right, Benjy?" she asked, genuinely concerned.

"Oh, Mom, everything is killin' me. My achin' stomach and my achin' head and my achin' feet."

"Well, my aching ears are killing me from hearing you complain so much," shouted Izzy, as he was being carried past his little brother.

"Anyway, Mom," Benjy continued, not paying any attention to Izzy, "did you see the way we mashed 'em. I gave him everything I had. Pow! Kapow! Zoom! I kicked him in the head...in the guts...in the ears...eyes...nose and throat. I kicked him where I'm not even allowed to say. I even threw my shoe at 'em. Pow! We were great, huh Mom?" Benjy wanted his mother's approval, and respect.

"I don't know what you were", Mrs. Gold angrily said, looking over at her husband, "but I do know that we are leaving here right now!"

Benjy was disappointed. Especially when his mother went to speak to his father. He didn't have to be told what they were discussing.

"Great," he said to himself, "just when we're having the most fun, we gotta go home."

Chapter 12
The Little Fibber

Inspector! Inspector Kohen!" Mr. Gold called, slowly walking back to the center of the parking lot where the inspector and his men were in animated conversation.

"Inspector Kohen, my wife and I have decided that we just cannot stay here any longer. I know you feel you can protect us from these terrorists, but I think that the best protection for us would be a short trip back to the States, at least until you catch these madmen."

"I'm afraid I have to agree with you, Mr. Gold," the inspector answered. "But let's talk about this inside the hotel. It's starting to really pour out here."

No one had noticed how overcast the sky had become until a sudden barrage of rainwater soaked everyone at once.

The waters of the Kinneret — the major reservoir for the area — seemed to reach up to the rain, anxious for the blessings that the rains of Israel gave. Little waves lapped up the millions of drops that fell. For too long now the drought that had plagued Israel, and the Galilee in particular, had drained the Kinneret of its life-giving fluid. But now the waters from above poured down, thrashing the land and swiftly adding liquid life to the Kinneret.

Once inside the hotel lobby, Inspector Kohen tried to reassure the Gold family.

"Tomorrow, first thing, we'll take you out of here and head straight to Ben Gurion Airport. I'll call the airport today and make all the arrangements."

"Can't we go today? Right now?" Mrs. Gold pleaded. "I hate to spend even one night here."

"It's getting dark, and the rains don't seem to be letting up. I think it would be safer if we waited until tomorrow," the inspector cautioned. He knew that in this rain they would be sitting ducks for an ambush.

"And also, Naomi," Mr. Gold added, "the children could use a good night's rest before going back on that long journey."

"I suppose you're right," his wife admitted, "but I'm so worried I just don't know what to do first. This is just a terrible, terrible nightmare." Simon saw his wife lose control even as she started to cry. Instantly, he was at her side, trying to comfort her. The inspector and his men felt a great wave of sympathy for this brave family.

"I'll have a guard stationed on the porch of your bungalow all night," the inspector assured them. "Don't worry, it will be all right." But his words sounded hollow, even to himself.

Simon didn't say anything. He just led his wife back to their bungalow. The inspector watched them go. Perhaps with the Golds safe in the United States, he might have a better chance at catching the terrorists. It was already the 11th of Ramadan. He had less than 24 hours to unravel the meaning of the "Secondary Target." There was always the chance that as long as the terrorists did not have their "Primary Target," a member of the Gold family for ransom, they might not even go after their secondary objective. But it was not a chance he was prepared to take.

The inspector saw his wife sitting not far away. She had been watching him and the Golds, and he knew she was probably upset at having been brought into the "war zone." He had promised a vacation. But he had given her terror and uncertainty instead. Slowly, he made his way over to her.

"Heftzi," he said softly, "I don't know what to say. It's going to be a long night, and I'm afraid not much of a vacation for either of us. But, I'll make it up...I promise I will." He couldn't help thinking how many promises he had made within the last few hours. Promises he was not sure he could keep.

"It's okay," his wife answered, getting up and trying to smile. "I suppose, seeing what that family has been going through I can't complain. But, at least we were able to sit and talk for three hours in the car, without interruption...almost.

"It's been a long day," she sighed, "and I don't have much of an appetite, so I'm going to turn in. Please be careful." She reached up and kissed him on the cheek. Without looking back, she went to their room.

The inspector watched Heftzi leave and then abruptly turned toward a group of policemen waiting for him. In a few moments he was lost in a discussion of security arrangements for the evening.

At supper, the Gold children, escorted by a policeman, entered the dining room. Mr. Gold had stayed behind, anxiously watching over his wife who was exhausted. There were about 30 other guests already in the dining room. Once the children were safely inside, the policeman took his place with the other guards, outside.

Ruth began feeding Rachel. Rebecca was peeling the crust off her bread, taking most of the soft inside away with it. She had already "cleaned" four slices of bread in this manner. What little there was left of each slice she quickly stuffed into her mouth. The waiter had tried to take her "piles of crust" away, but she had screamed so loudly, that he had quietly retreated to the other side of the dining room. Meanwhile, her "piles" were getting higher and higher with each new slice she cleaned.

Benjy was having the time of his life. He wasn't interested in food. Not when there was a room full of people who actually wanted to hear about his recent karate fight. Everyone had heard of the attack. Many were curious to find out the details of what Benjy billed "The Bloody Battle of the Century!" And, if it were details they wanted, he was their man.

"Here's what happened," he explained to a young couple who had invited him over to their table. They were newlyweds from England. The young bride thought Benjy was "an absolute dear."

"First, two attacked me," Benjy began, "one from behind, the other from the front. They thought they'd get me
with a high-low attack. Kapow! I back-kicked (he demonstrated, almost falling over), then, without putting my foot
down, I swung it forward and kicked the guy in front of
me. Bam! Smacked him right in the knee. Then — "

"Isn't he marvelous, Allan?" the young bride interrupted. "I do hope we have one just like him," she smiled,
blushing slightly.

"Yes, yes dear," her husband said only half paying
attention to her, "but let's hear what happened next," he
continued, truly caught up in the action.

"Yeah, as I was sayin', then a really big guy, with a
knife...yeah, a knife...and a sword," Benjy liked that extra
touch, and he could see that the young man was really
taking it in, "yeah, with a sword with a red handle,
and...and...a curved blade. This guy comes at me on a
horse."

"My word! Did you hear that, Amalya? A horse!" Allan
was almost feverish with excitement. "But how did he get
a horse?"

"How did he get a horse?" Benjy repeated, to give
himself a little time to come up with an answer. "No
problemo! He, er, hid it in the bushes until he needed it.
Anyway, he begins to gallop at me. My poor sister, Ruthy,
you see her over there." He pointed to Ruth. She saw
him, smiled, and motioned for him to return to their table.
Benjy had no interest in being anywhere but where he
was.

"Ruthy was lyin' down on the ground, blood coming out

of her head...and...uh...her ear. The guy was gonna run her over when — "

"He's such an absolute dear, Allan," Amalya interrupted again. "Look at the way his nose wiggles when he talks. That little lisp. That darling cleft in his chin. Oh, I do so hope we have one that looks like him."

"Yes, right away, dear," Allan agreed, holding up his hand in order to silence her.

Amalya became immediately insulted.

"I beg your pardon?" she blared at her husband. "Are you waving your hand at me? Are you trying to ignore me, Allan?" she cried out.

Allan, caught between Benjy's action-packed tale and his wife's anger, didn't know what to do. For the moment, he was speechless.

Benjy thought that was his cue to continue.

"Well, I took out my ninchucks (he grabbed Allan's napkin and twirled it around himself) and prepared to break the legs of the horse. I figured if I could time it just right, it would fall down before it stomped on Ruthy."

"My word, she looks awfully fit, for having had such a trouncing," Allan remarked, looking straight at Ruth and ignoring his wife's icy stare.

"Yeah, well the horse barely touched her. And, anyway, she's a quick healer. We all are," Benjy confided. "Why, once I broke this arm in six places and two days later it was as good as new," he said, holding up his right arm.

"My word, in six places!" Allan still failed to acknowledge Amalya's deadly stare.

"However did you manage that?" he asked, innocently. That was exactly what Benjy wanted.

"Well, that was when I saved Jake and...and...Becky, my other sister, over there, from the Indians."

"Indians?" Allan yelped, a bit bewildered by the new twist Benjy's story was taking.

"Yeah, in the States. The last wild tribe. The Kowabongas, I think they called 'em. They had war-paint and stuff and were getting ready to attack, when — "

"Allan Bartholomew Schtreimel!" Amalya finally exploded. She shot up from her seat. "I don't believe this! You actually believe this little fibber here, don't you? What a fool you are, Allan. And I? To think I thought you were so wonderful and clever. Why, we've only been married a week, and you're already ignoring me. And for what? Some silly, infantile story?"

"Hey!" Benjy said, ready to defend his story (depending on which one she attacked).

"But I thought you said he was such 'a dear,' Amalya," Allan suddenly found his voice. "Now, all of a sudden, everything he says is infantile. Well, let me tell you, I think he makes a lot more sense than you do some of the time."

Even as he spoke, Allan realized he had made a big mistake. Shocked by his outburst, Amalya turned white, tears cascading from her eyes. Abruptly, she turned and stalked out of the dining room. Allan hesitated for a moment, then, shouting "Amalya! Amalya dear! Please wait!" rushed out after her.

Benjy was a bit perplexed. He couldn't understand why

Allan would want to run after Amalya. Especially when he hadn't finished the best parts of either story. He shrugged, and began looking around for a new victim. He had just about made up his mind to go over to a nice old man sitting with his two grandchildren when a voice called out to him.

"Benjy!" Ruth shouted. "You come back here this minute. What are you doing?"

"Hey," Benjy said, walking slowly back to his table, "I was just telling — "

"You weren't telling, you were lying," scolded Ruth. "Now, you sit down and finish eating or, so help me, I'm going to tell Dad to give you the biggest spanking you ever had."

Benjy sat down with a "humpf." Just then Rebecca carefully balanced her seventh piece of crust on her pile. The baby, seeing this masterpiece, stretched out her hand and toppled the whole tower. Rebecca screamed. The baby, scared, screamed too, and soon they were both wailing.

"Now look what you've done!" yelled Ruth, looking right at Benjy.

"Me?" Benjy yelled back.

"Yes, you! Why did you have to go telling lies to everyone? I can't watch all of you at the same time. Now sit still. Eat!" she commanded, and then turned her attention to the two little ones.

Benjy, head bowed, looked into his plate. Tears began to form in his eyes. Ruth managed to quiet the children and then saw Benjy.

"Benjamin," she said softly.

"What?!" he barked.

"Come on, Benjy. It's just that when you make up stories like that, I get worried that you don't know yourself what is real and what is fake. Sometimes you get so caught up in one of your kung-fu tales, karate-chopping and kicking, that I wonder whether you know that what you're telling everyone is just made up."

"But I know," Benjy assured her, his eyes still on his plate. "So what?"

"Well, it's okay if you make up stories to entertain people. As long as you don't believe them yourself or do any damage by telling them. But you see what happened to that nice couple before. Now they have real problems, just because of your crazy stories."

"Hey, wait a minute," Benjy said, feeling that his sister had gone too far this time. "Is it my fault that guy believed me? He probably believes in the tooth fairy too!"

Ruth couldn't help but smile.

"Okay, never mind, let's clean up Rebecca and Rachel and see how the others are doing."

Suddenly, a bright bolt of lightning flashed through the sky. Benjy let out a little yelp. Rebecca cowered in her seat. Other people in the dining room were also startled.

The lights flickered and went out. The policemen quickly rushed in to protect the children. But, a moment later the lights went back on.

The manager of the hotel appeared and told everyone to return to their rooms. While he was talking, the lights began to flicker on and off again. The guests needed no further encouragement and began filing out of the dining room.

The kids ran from the dining room to their bungalow, their police escort trailing behind. By the time they got to their rooms, they were drenched.

Chapter 13
Giant Waves

When Mr. Gold heard the children returning, he crossed the little porch that connected their bungalows and entered the children's rooms.

"Hi, kids," he said. Everyone looked up.

"Hi, Dad," they mumbled.

"Quite a day we had today, huh?" Mr. Gold continued. "At this rate you guys should get credit toward your army enlistment. You sure are fighting enough." No one laughed. Jake tried a chuckle, just to be polite. They were all tired and the rain's constant clatter was just a little unnerving.

"Well, I spoke to the inspector," Mr. Gold tried again, "and we're going home tomorrow."

"Great!" Izzy said. "I never thought I would say this, Dad, but I can't wait to get back to school. At least there I get to fight people my own size."

This time everyone laughed.

"I think I should clarify myself," Mr. Gold said. "We're

not going home, that is, we're not going back to Jerusalem just yet. We're going on a short trip back to the States."

"Yippee!" shouted Benjy. "I'm going to see my best friend Solly again. Yippee!"

"That's great, Dad," Ruth added. "For how long?"

"A couple of weeks, I should think. Until things cool off."

"Or blow up," Jake suggested with a twinkle in his eye. They all laughed again.

Mr. Gold could see that everyone felt better now, more relieved. So, saying goodnight, he kissed each child and walked back to his room. Once there, he checked on his wife, who was sleeping soundly, and got ready for bed. He was tired. But his mind kept racing, creating terrible images of what might lie ahead. The more he tried to sleep, the worse the images got. Finally, in desperation, he took two sleeping pills. Slowly, the images began to fade, and he fell fast asleep.

Outside, the rains poured down continuously. The steady drone of the raindrops, the staccato tapping on the roof of the bungalow and the window panes, lulled everyone into a deep sleep. There was not even any wind to change the constant sound of a million wet fingers tapping everywhere.

The Kinneret drank in the water, built up its strength, and then, like a roaring tiger, broke the bonds that had kept it in its basin for so many years. The waters, at first hesitantly, reached over their banks. But, as more rain came down, the small waves turned into foaming tentacles, pushing and pulling at every living thing. The cats that made the kibbutzim and hotels their base, scurried for cover, but many drowned as the seething water caught up with them. Trees and bushes were ripped apart. The lone road leading to Tiberias disappeared beneath the bubbling waters.

The Shalom Hotel was a good fifty yards from the water's edge. A high bank, fully 10-feet tall, stretched between the last row of bungalows and the lake. The rising waters of the Kinneret slowly gathered at the base of this sand and stone barrier, methodically loosening the rocks and dissolving the sand. Leaks began appearing all across the barrier, and, as the holes grew larger, the water rushed in, eager to soak up more ground.

The Gold's bungalow was at the closest point to the bank. The inspector had felt it was safer to keep them as far away from the main hotel as possible. If there were another attack, the hotel and the bungalows closest to it would, he was sure, be hit first.

The water lapped at the front steps of the porch, reaching the first step, then the second, and finally up to the porch itself. Policewoman Rivka Shamgar was on duty, sitting on the porch that connected the children's room to that of their parents. Her Uzi submachine gun rested within easy reach by her side. The heavy rains had lulled her into a sort of half-sleep. She began to dream of her family. Of her brother who had fought in two wars and returned triumphant as a tank commander. In her dream she saw him fighting in the desert, his unit's tanks blazing fire at the enemy across the border. Slowly, they began moving forward, like great prehistoric dinosaurs trudging through the water. Water? she heard herself say. How did the tanks get into the water? They were in the desert. What was happening? The tanks were sinking... sinking...the water rising...her brother shouting to his men... to her...sinking...

Rivka awoke with a start. What a strange dream, she thought, and, at the same moment felt her shoes soaked with water. At first she thought she had stretched them out past the overhang covering the porch, but then she looked down. There was water lapping at her ankles. She looked out toward the lake, expecting to see the moonlight reflected on the still water. But instead, she saw giant waves forming, their crests within easy view.

"What's going on?" she said out loud. Those giant waves were not moving through the Kinneret; they were heading straight for the bungalow!

"Aieee!" she shouted and jumped out of her chair. The chair fell back with a bang as she began fiercely pounding on Mr. Gold's door. Standing there, she could see the water rushing underneath the door. She remembered the children and turned to their room. Again she began pounding, at the same time yelling for everyone to get up. She could hear the children stirring but no one was at the door yet. She looked out at the Kinneret. The waves were getting higher as they got closer. What to do? Break down the door? Run for help?

Suddenly the door on the other side opened. Mr. Gold, still groggy from the sleeping pills, stood in his pajamas, eyes fixed on the watery scene around him.

"My God, what's happened?" he called, trying to understand the situation and make himself heard above the rain.

"Quick," Rivka responded, "get the key to the children's room. We must get them away, up to dry land. Hurry!"

His head spinning, Mr. Gold ran back into his room. He woke his wife, grabbed the keys, and rushed to unlock the door of the sleeping children.

Once inside, he saw that the children were up, but in a frenzy. Some, stepping onto the floor, had felt the rising water. The little ones, seeing the older ones panic, started screaming hysterically. Mr. Gold tried to turn on the lights, but the electricity was out. Everyone was shouting. The water, as if in answer to their screams, came rushing in, higher and higher until it reached Benjy's knees.

"Help, Dad!" Benjy cried.

"Don't worry, I'm here, Benjy, I've got you," Ruth called back and ran to hold his hand.

"Quick, Jacob," Mr. Gold shouted, "grab Rachel and follow Rivka. I'll get Rebecca."

Sloshing their way to the little ones, Mr. Gold and Jake managed to get the children. Jake was having trouble with Rachel, who desperately wanted to go to her father. But Jake held her firmly and went to the policewoman. Ruth helped Benjy get out of the bungalow, and Mr. Gold came out with Rebecca. By this time, Mrs. Gold was outside herding everyone together.

As if on cue, the foundations of the bungalow started to shift. The waves began pounding the wall with new

Those giant waves were not moving through the Kinneret;
they were heading straight for the bungalow!

strength. The water was now almost thigh-deep on Mr. Gold.

Varoom! One side of the bungalow caved in.

"Hurry!" cried Mr. Gold. "Everyone follow me!" He swiftly took the lead, trudging up toward the hotel. As they passed the side of their bungalow they heard another crash, as the front porch was washed away.

Halfway to the hotel, Mrs. Gold suddenly turned to her husband and shouted, "Where's Isaac?"

"Isaac?" Mr. Gold repeated, bewildered for a second. "Oh no! Isaac! Isaac!" he began to shout, looking toward the bungalow.

By this time Rivka, who was in the rear, had reached Mr. Gold. She was concerned that they were going too slowly. But, before she could protest, Mr. Gold shouted out.

"We're missing one child!"

"Okay, I will go look for him," she said.

"No, take Rebecca, I'll go." Mr. Gold shoved Rebecca into Rivka's hands and moved off. "Hurry!" he shouted behind him. "Take them to high ground."

Mrs. Gold called out, but no one could hear her over the rain and the noise of the collapsing bungalows. She began feeling sharp pains in her stomach and it was getting harder and harder for her to walk.

Inch by inch the group made their way to the hotel. Before long, three policemen, sent by the inspector to see what was happening to the Golds, reached them and helped them to safety. Once inside, Mrs. Gold turned to go back to her husband. Gentle hands restrained her.

"Please, Mrs. Gold, stay here." It was Heftzi, the inspector's wife. "The children need you. You can't help your husband right now and, worse yet, something may happen to you and your baby. Please, please, stay here. My husband has already gone out to help Mr. Gold find your child."

"But Isaac," Mrs. Gold sobbed. Then, gathering some inner strength, she turned to her children, commanding some men standing nearby to "get some towels and blankets for the children."

Only after she was sure the children were out of their wet clothes and more or less comfortable did she look out of the big glass window of the hotel, toward her bungalow.

She could barely make out the remains of the building, but she thought she saw her husband and...and...someone else? Could it be? Could he have found Isaac?

Chapter 14
Kidnapped!

Just 15 minutes before policewoman Rivka began pounding on the children's door, Mohammed Shoukary slowly pried open the sliding glass door in the rear of their bungalow. Shoukary was a terrorist who had been in Israeli hands before, but was traded, along with 400 others, for the bodies of two Israelis missing in action.

Once inside, Shoukary took out his knife. Rebecca stirred, mumbling something in her sleep. The terrorist froze for a moment, ready to pounce. He listened intently for any sounds of movement. But all he heard was the steady patter of the rain.

He had his orders. No killing. Just take one hostage. Just one. That would be enough.

Isaac, sleeping closest to the sliding door, sensed a presence in the room. Perhaps it was the shadow of the terrorist falling across his face. Perhaps it was the cool air that blew in from the door left ajar. Whatever it was, it made Isaac wake up with a start. He sat up and looked straight into the eyes of the intruder. At first he thought it was a dream. But, when he saw the knife glimmering in the moonlight, he knew this was no dream. This was a real, live nightmare!

He opened his mouth to scream, but Shoukary was already upon him. With his knife hand Shoukary lifted Isaac off the bed, the other hand securely covering his mouth and nose. Isaac tried desperately to kick and squirm his way out. But he was caught, his arms pinned across his chest, as though he was in a straitjacket. Worse still, the hand over his face was cutting off his air supply. He needed air. Air! But as he kicked and turned, the giant hand only closed tighter and tighter...tighter and tighter...until finally Isaac passed out. Shoukary quickly left the room with his prize and transferred Isaac to the waiting hands of another terrorist.

Mr. Gold sloshed his way back to the bungalow, but he could see that the situation was all but hopeless. The bungalow had caved in, leaving just one wall standing. His only hope was that somehow Isaac had gotten out in time. If he was in that pile of rubble...

Shouting "Isaac!" at the top of his lungs, Mr. Gold began to search for his son. The rain was still coming down in buckets and all but drowned out his calls. He was about to return to the hotel to get help when he thought he saw something move just to the right of him. He turned to see what is was, but the sheets of rain made visibility almost zero. He stared into the darkness. Suddenly, he was attacked head-on by someone with terrific strength.

Mr. Gold tried to flip the other man, but he couldn't

keep his balance long enough to get the leverage he needed. The rain made the ground too slippery. Simon started sliding and the attacker saw his chance. He smacked his fist, hard, into Mr. Gold's stomach. Mr. Gold doubled over in pain and backed off, trying hard to catch his breath. As the attacker came to deliver another blow, Simon shot forward and shoved his body into the attacker. Both of them went down.

The assailant managed to get on top of Mr. Gold, and started punching him mercilessly. Mr. Gold rolled, throwing his attacker off. They grappled, the water almost drowning them both. Mr. Gold felt himself begin to lose consciousness as calloused fingers found his throat and began squeezing. They kept pressing and pressing, holding his head under the rising water. But just then he sensed, more than saw, another person join the battle. The attacker let go and Mr.Gold felt himself being lifted up. "Easy, Mr. Gold, I've got you," a familiar voice said. It was the inspector. He had his gun trained on the attacker as he helped Mr. Gold steady himself.

"Move!" he commanded the terrorist, pushing him up the hill. "Move!" he shouted again, throwing the man into the water. The terrorist was slow to get up and the inspector grabbed him by the back of his shirt, lifted him and shoved him forward. The terrorist fell down, too weak to get up.

"Help me with him," the inspector commanded Mr. Gold. Together, they dragged the attacker back to the hotel.

Chapter 15
Smell That Chicken Soup

Isaac awoke to find himself lying on the back seat of a small automobile. Afraid to get up, he half-opened his eyes, very slowly. There were two men in the front of the car. They were speaking Arabic, but he sensed that they were nervous about something.

The little Fiat was perched precariously on the edge of the road, or what was left of it. Straight down was a 100-foot drop. One terrorist was screaming at the other for getting them into such a predicament.

After a while, the two men got out of the car and walked a few feet away. Isaac peeked out of the window. He saw the steep drop and fell back on his seat, overwhelmed by a feeling of impending doom. He was sure they were going to kill him and push the car over the cliff. But actually this was the furthest thing from their minds. They had been ordered to guard Isaac from harm. Yakub had made that quite clear. What they hoped to do was push the car back onto the main surface of the road.

This is it, Isaac told himself. I'm dead. And for what? A stupid message which I didn't understand anyway.

I wonder if the others will remember me. Oh sure, Jake and Ruthy will remember me as a pretty great brother, and even Benjy may remember me, but — and now tears started running down his cheeks — Rebecca and little Rachel will never get to know what a great brother I am. They'll forget me. Even though it was me who diapered Rachel every morning when she got up. And it was me who gave both of them cereal. And it was me, me who played with them while everyone else was getting dressed. I know they'll forget me. I know it. How could they? He started to cry. The terrorists began rocking the car back and forth, trying to free it from the mud. Isaac, of course, felt sure that they were getting ready to push the car over the edge. He sat up, saw them straining against the car, and decided to make his move.

In one swift motion, he opened the door on the cliff side, and jumped out. The noise of the rain easily covered the click of the door opening. He fell a few feet and then managed to stop himself. It was a long way down. He lay flat against the ground, the car moving back and forth not far from his head.

Isaac realized he had to make a run for it. If the car fell now, it would crush him. So, pushing himself off the ground, he started to run-slide-roll down the cliff.

The terrorists, unable to see or hear anything in the driving rain, continued to rock the car until it was free. Then they carefully pushed it up onto higher ground. Soaked, and annoyed by the delay, they jumped into the car and took off. They drove for about half a mile before the one on the passenger side decided to see how their captive was doing. When he turned around his face dropped. Isaac, of course, was not there. He told his partner to stop and back up but the road behind them was completely washed out.

With little choice left, they proceeded to their rendezvous point with Yakub. Neither spoke. Each was thinking of how they could blame the other for losing their hostage...and allowing their leader, Shoukary, to be captured.

Meanwhile, Isaac had landed at the bottom of the cliff in a water-logged ravine. The mud cushioned his fall, saving him from any serious injuries. In a way, he felt happy, congratulating himself on a skillful escape. But, when he finally realized that the terrorists had not pushed the car over the side of the road, he began to worry. Left alone, drenched, in only his pajamas, there was a good chance he might die of exposure. He had to get back to the hotel.

Exhausted, Isaac pulled himself up, inch by inch, until he reached the road. By now the first rays of dawn had begun to appear and the rain was letting up. But where was the hotel? he asked himself. He could barely make out the road itself. Keeping the cliff to his right he slowly trudged on. In some places the water was knee-deep, almost sweeping him off his feet. Eventually, he was able to make out some dim lights and buildings about a quarter of a mile away.

"Hurray!" he yelled. He didn't much care if it was the

hotel or not. As long as it was warm and he could call his parents. His fingernails were badly broken and his face and hands were caked in mud. It was impossible to make out the bright blue football helmets that decorated his now torn pajamas. Mud, dirt, leaves and grass covered him from head to toe.

As the sunlight became stronger and the rain stopped entirely, Isaac realized how tired he was. The short distance that lay between him and the houses ahead seemed uncrossable, and he began to doubt whether he would make it.

"Oh, no," he moaned, "what a way to go. Just before I get to the safety of those warm houses, I'm going to drop dead. That's really beautiful. I'm going to fall over dead at the doorstep of some Israeli family and miss all the chicken soup they would probably give me to warm myself up. Then, this kind family would probably drive me back to the hotel. Everyone would bundle me up and take me home. Mom would make tons of southern fried chicken until I got my strength back. And no school! Why, I wouldn't have to go to school for days, maybe weeks. Hey, in my condition, I might have to miss the whole rest of the year!" Isaac's eyes lit up. He was determined not to drop dead.

With new resolve, Isaac began pushing himself forward toward the glistening lights. He reached the nearest house and, using his last ounce of strength, burst in, almost able to smell the chicken soup. But no one was home. The house was empty. Isaac suddenly realized that what he had thought was light coming from inside the houses had actually been the sun's rays reflecting off the wet windows. Crushed, Isaac sat down on the floor and started to cry.

"It's not fair," he told himself, pounding on the floor, "I want chicken soup!"

Chapter 16
"Don't Shoot!"

Mohammed Shoukary slowly came to his senses. He was in a room in the hotel. He knew that those around him were waiting for him to open his eyes. He also knew that his attempt to capture Mr. Gold, the man his superiors really wanted — had failed. At least his men had the child. Now, all he had to do was wait. His brothers had always found a way to set him free. They would find a way again.

He kept his eyes closed. Let them wait, he thought.

Whack! Mohammed felt a hot pain across his right cheek. Whack! Now his left cheek burned. He opened his eyes with a start.

"I thought that might wake you up," Inspector Kohen said in perfect Arabic. "Now, if you've stopped playing games, I think we should have a little talk."

The other officers in the room were silent. They knew the procedure. And they waited.

Mohammed just looked at the inspector. No trace of emotion in his face.

Whack! "That's just to jog your memory, and so you understand we mean business," the inspector snarled. "Now, what was your mission and who is your contact?"

Mohammed did not answer.

Inspector Kohen moved toward Mohammed, as if to hit him again. This time the terrorist let out a little yelp and cringed.

"Talk," the inspector shouted, grabbing Shoukary by his shirt.

This time Mohammed tilted his head toward Mr. Gold who had been watching the interrogation. In a low voice he said, "My mission was to kidnap that person and to report my success to my brothers waiting in a car not far away."

"Are they the ones who have the boy?" the inspector asked.

"Yes."

"And what were you to do after you captured this man?"

"Await further orders."

"From whom?"

"We were not told. All I knew is that I would be contacted."

Whack! The inspector hit Mohammed again. And before the Arab could regain his composure, whack! He hit him once more.

"Again I ask you, from whom?" the inspector said in a cold menacing tone.

"I—I do not know," the Arab yelled, fear evident in his eyes.

At this point Simon Gold walked out. He couldn't believe what he had just witnessed. The kind, helpful inspector he thought he knew, had turned into something wild and ferocious. Quite possibly, he might kill the Arab. Simon didn't want to see it. At the same time he really didn't care what it took to find out where they had taken his son. As long as they found out.

The inspector, meanwhile, saw that Mohammed would say no more. He left one of his men with the terrorist and walked outside.

"Mr. Gold!" Shlomo said as he approached Simon. "I don't think this fellow knows where your son is. He is only a hired thug. But one thing is for sure. We cannot waste any more time. We must get you and your family to the airport and out of the country."

"What?" Simon exclaimed. "Do you think we would leave Israel without our son? Are you completely crazy? We don't leave until Isaac is found. And that's final!"

"But then you run the risk of further endangering the rest of your family. Do you want that?"

"You may be right," Mr. Gold acknowledged, "but it doesn't change the fact that we are not leaving Israel without our son."

"We'll discuss this later," the inspector said, hoping to come up with a way of convincing Mr. Gold that he had to leave now. There was always force, but only as a last resort.

"Fine," Simon answered, "but the answer will remain the same. We're staying until Isaac is with us."

He turned and began walking to his wife.

Just then there was a terrible commotion at the front door of the hotel. Everyone ran outside.

There, muddy and tired, stood Isaac. He was exhausted, having travelled in circles before finding the road leading to the hotel. His eyes were fixed on the ground in front of him. He could barely move. Somehow, the thought of all that chicken soup and missing all that school had kept him going.

When he heard the yells of everyone coming to greet him, he looked up. In front of him he saw half a dozen policemen with machine guns. He was sure they were going to shoot him.

"Oh, no!" he screamed. "Don't shoot! Don't shoot!" he pleaded. "Look, it's me, Izzy, Isaac, Isaac Gold! Oh, no! I don't believe it. Shot by our side! Help! Helllp!" he began to shout as he fell to the ground and started to wail.

The Gold family ran over to Isaac, who continued to yell, "Don't shoot! Don't shoot!"

"Izzy, you're not dead, honest. You're not dead!" Benjy said to his brother.

But Izzy didn't or wouldn't hear him. He just kept shouting, "Don't shoot!" as his father carried him to the hotel lobby.

After Izzy was settled comfortably in a room, the inspector spoke to Mr. Gold.

"I've had my men bring in a special ATV to get you and your family out of here. In two hours we are leaving for the airport, even if I have to tie you all up and dump you into the plane."

Mr. Gold shook Shlomo's hand. "You'll get no argument from me, Inspector. U.S.A., here we come." And he ran to tell his wife and children.

Chapter 17
The Battle of Babel

By noon Inspector Kohen and his wife, together with the entire Gold clan were ready to go to the airport. He would be using only vehicles designed for the difficult ride that they would face after yesterday's rains. The roads were too washed out for anyone to follow them. For once, the inspector felt he had things pretty well under control. Of course, he hadn't figured on the little terrorist within their ranks. Benjamin Gold, a.k.a. Benjy.

It happened during lunch.

"I want everyone to eat a big meal," Mr. Gold announced. "I'm telling everyone now, there will be no stopping on the way to the airport. We've got a three-hour trip ahead of us and the inspector and his men are in no mood for any shenanigans. For that matter, neither am I. Okay?" Simon Gold looked around to make sure everyone understood. They were all tense from lack of sleep and their early morning adventure. But even Isaac had made it for lunch, too nervous to sleep and too scared to stay by himself in his room.

They marched into the dining room.

"Hi, Allan!" Benjy suddenly shouted, waving excitedly. Allan Schtreimel looked up and saw his worst friend, Benjy. Allan's first inclination was to wave back in greeting, but one look from Amalya quickly changed his mind. Instead, he gave Benjy a half-smile and turned back to his food.

"Who's your friend, Benjy?" his father asked.

"Just a nice guy I met yesterday. We became friends after I told him about my kung-fu battles." Benjy took pride in the fact that an adult was his friend. "But to tell you the truth, Dad," he continued, "Allan isn't all that smart, if you know what I mean. He believed everything I said. Even about the Indians."

"Indians?" his father said, astonished.

"Don't ask, Dad," Ruth cut in. "You'll notice that Allan and his new bride are not overwhelmed with joy at seeing Benjy. That's because — "

"Hey," Benjy interrupted, insulted by Ruth's remark. "What do you mean they're not over...over whatever it was you said. They are so over it. Look, I'll show you." Before they could stop him, Benjy raced over to Allan's table.

The Schtreimels were still not on the best of terms with each other, although the iciness between them was slowly beginning to thaw. Allan had continued to apologize all the way back to their room, but, as his wife said, he was in the "dog house." They had skipped breakfast and tried to talk things through. So they had no knowledge of the morning's events.

Benjy was determined to remedy that.

"Hi, Allan," Benjy smiled, hoping his father was watching.

"Hi, Mrs. Allan," he continued, unaware that she was ignoring him. "Well, you probably want to hear what happened to me this morning, huh?"

"Uh, no, Benjy, but thanks anyway," Allan said, feeling very uncomfortable. "We're in a bit of a rush now, so why don't you and I get together later and you can tell me all the stories you want?" Allan hoped Benjy would take the hint.

"Oh, I can't do that Allan. We're going to the airport soon. See those men," Benjy pointed to the guards near his table at the door. "They're our security detail. They're here to make sure the terrorists don't attack us again."

Amalya looked at Benjy. Sparks of hatred shot out from her eyes. Allan saw the storm clouds looming closer and tried desperately to dismiss Benjy.

"Yes, well, Benjy, now's just not a good time." He made ready to get up, hoping Amalya, and not Benjy, would follow him.

"But this is the truth," protested Benjy. "My brother, Izzy, almost died yesterday. Those terrorists kidnapped him and —"

"That's it! I have had enough!" Amalya blurted out, no longer able to restrain herself. "Listen young man, I want you to stop your fibbing this instant. We are not interested in your lies!"

Benjy felt tears fill his eyes. This time he was telling

the truth and he would defend his story to the death.

"But I'm not lying. Ask Izzy. Ask the security men. Ask — "

"What seems to be the trouble?" Mr. Gold inquired as he walked over to the Schtreimel's table. "Is Benjy annoying you?"

"Well, no, not real — " began Allan.

"He most certainly is," interrupted his wife. "This little fibber has been spinning one silly tale after another. He absolutely insists on disturbing us every chance he gets. It's become so we can't eat a meal in peace." By this time Amalya was out of her chair, screaming.

Mr. Gold was upset. He didn't like Benjy telling tales. But, he didn't like the way this woman was talking about his son.

"I understand you are upset, but Benjy meant no harm. Apologize, Benjamin, and let's get going."

"I will not!" Benjy declared, barely able to hold back his tears. "I was just telling them the truth about the terrorists."

"Oh please," Amalya taunted, showing utter contempt.

"But it's true, if he talked about terrorists trying to kill us," Mr. Gold said.

"Not you too!" Amalya shouted. "Now I know where that fibber gets all his insane stories from." Before Mr. Gold could answer, Amalya turned and walked out the dining room.

Allan didn't know what to do. He got up to leave but, as he did so, his wife shouted back to him, "No, you stay here with these maniacs. Don't you dare come near me."

Not knowing whether to sit down or stand up and follow his wife, Allan hung in mid-air, half-sitting, half-stand-
ing. A waiter tried to squeeze between Allan's chair and
the one behind him. But just at that moment, Allan made
up his mind to follow his wife and moved his chair back.
The waiter promptly tripped over the chair and fell, tray
and all, bringing Allan down with him.

Eggs, cheese and jam splattered across the table of a
group of Japanese tourists. They jumped out of their
chairs and started shouting, as Allan and the waiter became hopelessly entangled on the floor.

The security guards, sure that this was part of a new
terrorist attack, quickly took out their guns and headed for
the mass of screaming people.

Seeing the guns held high, some people ran toward
the doors, while others dove under tables.

Only the Gold family remained seated. They continued
to eat as though nothing was happening. Rebecca, thinking that now would be a good time to show off some of
her musical repertoire, called for everyone to be quiet so
she could sing. Getting no positive response, she stood
on her chair and began a selection from her latest video
favorite, My Fair Lady. The other children laughed hysterically as Rebecca sang, "The Rain in Pain is Mainly Plain,"
her interpretation of "The Rain in Spain Falls Mainly on
the Plain."

Simon Gold began to separate Allan and the waiter.
Amalya, hearing the commotion, ran back into the dining
room. There, she saw Mr. Gold tugging at her husband
and assumed he was beating him. She immediately ran

...she stood on her chair and began a selection from her latest video favorite, My Fair Lady.

over to Mr. Gold and started hitting him with her fists, shouting, "Leave my husband alone, you bully!" Benjy, seeing his father attacked, carefully made his way over to Amalya and kicked her in the shins. He then raced back to the safety of his mother.

The guards, meanwhile, their guns still in the air, were shouting for everyone to sit down. Not understanding any Hebrew, the Japanese were sure they were being attacked and began shouting and kicking anyone within reach.

Allan, having almost reached an upright position, fell back onto the floor as Mr. Gold tried to fend off Amalya. The poor waiter was slowly being trampled under the feet of the high-kicking Japanese.

When Inspector Kohen arrived, he was confronted by a scene out of the Tower of Babel. Foreign tourists were cursing in Japanese, policemen were shouting in Hebrew, and a crazy woman was fighting with Mr. Gold, yelling in English.

By now a nice-sized crowd had gathered just beyond the open doors of the dining room, some of them yelling encouragement to the combatants inside. Wailing police sirens could be heard in the background.

Desperate, Inspector Kohen did something he had not done in over three years. He shot his gun in the line of duty. In the air, of course.

Everyone came to an immediate, and silent, stop.

"All of you, find your seats right now," the inspector commanded.

Everyone found a vacant seat.

"I am Inspector Kohen," he informed them. "I don't know what happened here, and I don't care. But I do want everyone, except for the Gold family, to remain in their seats. I tell you now, if anyone else moves, I will not be responsible for the consequences. All right. Will the Gold family please leave the dining room. Quickly."

Simon and Naomi led their children, under guard, out of the dining room.

"Now, the rest of you, finish your lunch and go about your business." The inspector signalled his men to follow as he walked out. In the background the voice of Amalya could be heard saying, as she gently wiped her husband's forehead, "There now, darling, everything will be all right. They're certain to lock up that crazy family once and for all."

"But...but..." her husband protested.

"Don't say a thing, dear," Amalya said. "I'll take care of you."

On their way out, the inspector asked Simon what happened.

"I'm not quite sure, Inspector," Simon answered, looking over at Benjy. "Maybe Benjy can explain."

No one had to ask Benjy twice.

"Well, it was like this, Inspector," he began. "This guy's wife took out a knife and attacked me. My father karated her hand, Pow! Kapow! and the knife fell. But she had some ninchucks and began smashing my hand. Dad tried to protect me, but she got him, so I kicked her real hard in the —"

"Never mind, Benjy," the inspector sighed, "I'll get one

of my men to take your statements."

"No problemo," Benjy happily agreed.

Inspector Kohen resigned himself to never finding out the truth.

Chapter 18
A Gold Tooth

At Ben Gurion Airport, Inspector Kohen personally helped clear all the luggage. The Golds waited in the safari jeep at a special, heavily guarded security zone at the edge of the airport. Their car would be brought back to Jerusalem from Tiberias when the roads cleared.

The jeep was big, but barely big enough for the whole family. Mr. Gold and his wife were having a difficult time controlling the children. Everyone was restless and anxious to stretch their legs. But the inspector's orders were clear. No one, under any circumstances, was allowed to leave the jeep.

"I only wish he could know what it's like having six children and a pregnant wife unable to get to the bathroom for almost three hours," Simon lamented.

"What did you say, dear?" his wife asked, fidgeting in her seat.

"Just that I wish the inspector would get us on the plane already."

"I wish he would get us to a bathroom," Naomi mumbled.

"Yes," Rebecca joined in, "I want to go to the bathroom to make my pee-pee."

"Me too!" the others chimed in.

"Well, you'll all have to wait until the inspector returns and we board the plane," Mr. Gold shouted, short-tempered and irritated at the constant whining in the car.

"Not me," announced Rebecca, "I need to pee-pee now."

"Great! Just great!" moaned Mr. Gold.

"Wonderful!" added Rebecca, failing to catch his sarcasm.

"Someone put a Pamper on her!" Mrs. Gold ordered. Izzy reached over to the back of the jeep and pulled out a Pamper. After a minor battle with his little sister, he managed to get it on her.

"Sit down, Benjamin," Simon spat between clenched teeth.

"I can't, I have to go." Benjy answered.

"Okay, someone put a Pamper on Benjy," his father yelled.

"Oh no, c'mon Dad," Benjy pleaded, not sure if his father was serious or not.

Izzy, meanwhile, went to get another Pamper. So did Jake.

"Here, Ruthy, why don't you take a Pamper for yourself," Jake said laughing.

"Oh yeah," she answered, reaching over for one. "Try this on for size," and she threw it at him.

Benjy, seeing he was missing all the fun, grabbed the Pamper out of Jake's hand and threw it at Izzy.

Rebecca wanted to play too. She took off her Pamper and threw it at Rachel. Her aim, however, was off by just a bit as the Pamper landed right on the top of Mr. Gold's head.

Simon was ready to explode, and indeed, he might have, had not a knock on the jeep window distracted him. It was the inspector.

"Hurry now, follow the lead car onto the airport runway. I've just received word that there was an explosion at the Shalom Hotel. That means the terrorists have not given up yet.

"Oh, and by the way," the inspector added, looking at the kids covered with Pampers and at the one on Mr. Gold's head, "I don't think you're supposed to put Pampers on that way," he finished with a smile.

Simon was not amused. He threw off the Pamper, muttering to himself, and followed the lead car onto the runway. Within minutes an El Al 747 taxied toward them and stopped only a few yards from the car. The doors of the plane opened as a mobile stairway was brought over.

"All right, everyone out," a secret-service man ordered.

"Please don't waste any time. Go as fast as you can into the plane and make sure you all stay together."

Everyone rushed out. The family was herded onto the plane. Once inside, they were ushered up another flight of steps into the first-class cabin. Two security guards accompanied them.

When the kids saw the spacious cabin, they were awed.

"Gee, this is super," Izzy said. "Look at the size of these seats, and the carpeting. This is living!"

"But I don't see what's so good about first class," Ruth complained. "Besides the seats, why would anyone want to pay more for first class?"

"Well, why don't you wait and see, dear?" Mrs. Gold said.

"Anyway," Jake added, straight-faced, "I hear that first class gets to land first."

"What?" Ruth exclaimed.

"Wow! We get to land first!" Benjy shouted. He ran down the aisle to tell the others the good news.

"Come on," Ruth said, unconvinced. "You can fool him, but you can't fool me. What do you mean, we land first?" Jake looked at her as if to say, "Don't you know anything?" Which prompted her to ask, "Okay, smarty, if you know so much, then answer this: How much earlier do we land?" She had him now.

"About an hour before the others," he immediately answered. "That way we're already off the plane before the rest of the people even get there."

"Dad!" Ruth called out to her father who was nearby. He had heard the entire conversation.

"Dad! I think Jake is teasing me. Tell him to stop."

"You heard your sister, Jake, stop pulling her leg," Mr. Gold admonished his son. "You know very well that first class lands not more than fifteen minutes earlier than the rest of the plane." Not waiting for a response, Mr. Gold walked down the aisle.

For a minute, Ruth didn't know what to think. Then she

"*Oh, and by the way,*" *the inspector added, looking at the kids covered with Pampers and at the one on Mr. Gold's head, "*I don't think you're supposed to put Pampers on that way.*"

heard her father laughing. Jake couldn't hold back any longer, and he started to laugh as well. Ruth joined in, good-naturedly, as if to say, "I knew you were joking all along."

By this time the other first-class passengers had started boarding. All told, five more passengers entered the first-class cabin, none with children. Indeed, most of the new passengers seemed a bit annoyed at the prospect of travelling eleven hours with six obviously overactive children. Especially, since they all seemed to be forever lined up at the lavatories.

An old man, with a white beard and thick bushy eyebrows, mumbled, "Leave it to El Al," as the no smoking/fasten your seat belt sign came on.

The children began arguing over window seats. Benjy tried to convince Izzy to let him sit near the window, "so I can see how much earlier we land." Jake and Ruth agreed to switch seats every hour so that they would each get a chance to see out the window. Rebecca and Rachel had seats too, but preferred to sit on Jake and Ruth. Mr. and Mrs. Gold sat in the next-to-the-last row, trying to keep everyone quiet.

Among the four remaining passengers was a couple in their late twenties. They alone, of all the passengers, seemed to enjoy the presence of the children in the cabin. Benjy, never one to waste time when he saw a likely candidate for his kung-fu stories, went over to the man and introduced himself.

"Hi, I'm Benjy," he said, fairly licking his lips in anticipation.

"Hi, Benjy, I'm Abraham. You can call me Abe. This is my wife, Iris."

"Hello, Benjy, is that your family?" Iris asked, pointing to the others.

"Sure is," Benjy answered proudly. "My mother over there is really not so fat. She's just expecting a baby. But we've been so busy lately fighting terrorists and kidnappers, she hasn't had time to have the baby yet." Benjy hoped he had whet their appetite for more information.

"I'm sorry, young man," a stewardess interrupted, "but the seat-belt sign is on. You'll have to get into your seat." She ushered him to his seat before he could protest. Gloomily, he folded his hands, planning his next tall-tale attack.

A blonde, Scandinavian looking woman sat down in front of Benjy. Her light hair and blue eyes intrigued him, and he couldn't wait to ask her if she was wearing a wig. But, before he could lean forward, a strong hand squeezed his shoulder.

"Whatever you're going to tell that woman, I don't care how important you think it is, I have one word of advice for you," Mr. Gold whispered into Benjy's ear. "Don't!"

This successfully dampened Benjy's desire for conversation. For the time being.

Mr. Gold had noticed the blonde woman also. But what caught his eye was the bright gold tooth she had near the front of her mouth. Russian, he thought.

The remaining passenger was a man in a three-piece business suit. His dark complexion and moustache indicated he was an Israeli, of perhaps Sephardic background. It was easy to tell that he was clearly uncomfortable in the suit, and would probably have been more at home in a T-shirt on a kibbutz. He carried an attache case and kept looking at the other passengers as though searching for the face of a friend. The plainclothes security men, sitting in the last row behind the family, quickly spotted the nervous man and made mental notes to watch him carefully.

As the engines started revving for take-off, Rachel began to cry. Jake, who had been in charge of her, quickly passed her back to his mother. With lift-off, Mrs. Gold began to feel the first stirrings of nausea. She swiftly handed the crying child to her husband while leaning forward in search of an air-sickness bag. A haggard-looking Simon Gold silently wished that first class would land hours before the rest of the plane.

After what seemed like an eternity of plugged ears and churning stomachs, the children felt the plane level off. Two minutes later the seat-belt sign blinked out.

The man with the attache case got up and quickly made his way to the bathroom, the case held firmly in his right hand. When he closed the lavatory door, the security guards got up and stood in front of the door. One guard had his hand inside his jacket, the other stood a little further away, at the ready.

As the guard knocked on the bathroom door, a painfully loud shot rang out.

Chapter 19
Skyjackers On Board

Everyone in the first-class cabin turned around. The guards had their guns out, but the shot had not come from the cabin. It had come from the coach section below.

In a flash, the two guards ran down the spiral staircase. Downstairs everyone was shouting and yelling at the same time. A man with a pistol was in one of the aisles, forcing people to stay in their seats. In the other aisle a woman holding a knife in one hand and a grenade in the other, was shouting at one of the passengers who had a deep gash on the side of his head. His wife was crying and yelling at the woman to leave her husband alone, protecting him with her body.

The two guards needed only seconds to assess the situation. But, before they could react, a voice from behind them said, "Unless you both want to die this instant, drop your guns and raise your hands above your heads."

Caught by surprise, they did as they were told.

It was the man with the attache case. He ordered them

to go back to the first-class cabin.

Once upstairs, the man forced the guards toward the front of the plane. He shoved them onto the floor. When one of the guards resisted, the hijacker slammed his pistol down, hitting the guard behind the head. He then tied both of the men up.

No one said a word. Abe and Iris, the couple who had talked to Benjy, held each other tightly. The old man with the beard attempted to get up, as if to protest, but when the terrorist pointed a gun in his direction, he sat down.

The woman hijacker came upstairs.

"We are all set," she said in broken English. "The captain refuses to let us into the cockpit. I have told him what will happen to the passengers if he does not obey us, but he still refuses to let us in."

"It makes little difference," the man in the suit said in near-perfect English. Carefully he took off his tie and jacket and opened his collar. "For now, let us consolidate our position. Wire the plane as planned and warn the pilot that if he attempts to land without our permission, we will blow up the aircraft."

Mr. Gold silently prayed that the children would not attract attention to themselves. It all seemed like a never-ending nightmare.

Naomi Gold suddenly raised her hand. The hijacker was even more amazed than Simon to see this.

"What is it?" he hissed.

"I must go to the ladies' room," Naomi pleaded. "I—I don't feel so well."

The man saw that she was pregnant. He motioned to

the woman to take Mrs. Gold to the lavatory.

Once there, the woman called out, "Yakub, come here. Quickly!" Hearing the word "Yakub," Mr. Gold instantly realized who this man was — the dreaded Yakub mentioned in the message!

"Oh, no," Simon moaned under his breath. He watched as Yakub walked over to the woman he called Jamaya and started an animated conversation. Mr. Gold was sure they were discussing his wife. If she was going into labor now, she would need him. But if he got up, one of the terrorists might misinterpret his move and shoot him. Dead, he would be of no use to anyone.

Jamaya came over to Mr. Gold and motioned him to go to his wife.

Ruth pleaded with her father not to go. She was afraid she would not see either of her parents again.

"Look, gang, I've got to help your mother. Jake, you and Ruth are in charge. Don't worry, I'll be back soon."

Then, trying hard to hold down his own growing fears, Simon rushed to the lavatory.

Inside, he found his wife propped against one of the walls of the tiny cubicle.

"Contractions," she managed to whisper, between harsh breaths. "I'm going into labor."

Mr. Gold turned to confront Yakub.

"Look, I don't care who you are or what you want. My wife is going into labor. She needs a doctor and proper facilities. You must land this plane at once."

"We do not land," Yakub flatly stated, allowing for no discussion. "Jamaya will get a stewardess. She will help you." Then he walked out.

Jamaya returned with a stewardess while Simon was trying to make his wife more comfortable.

"My name is Leah," she said as she entered the cramped compartment.

"Okay, Leah," Mr. Gold said, keeping his eye on his wife. "My wife is having our seventh child. I don't know how long the contractions will last. Sometimes it takes quite a few hours; sometimes she gives birth shortly after her first contraction. I need lots of towels and any sheets you may have around. Get me some ice chips too."

Leah left to get whatever she could.

"Simon," his wife called out to him, in obvious pain. "Don't go anywhere. You've got to help me through this."

"I know dear," he answered her, trying to sound calm. "You just keep up your breathing exercises. Leah went to get the things we may need."

"You mean they won't land the plane?" Simon could hear a note of terror in her voice.

"Of course they will," he lied, "but just in case, I want to be prepared. Remember how fast you had Izzy? I only had one shoe on for the delivery." Simon laughed. His wife was too involved in an oncoming contraction to do anything but breathe.

Back in the cabin, it dawned on Jake and Ruth that as of now they were both father and mother to the other children. Normally, that would have been fun. Now, however, the responsibility was awesome.

Suddenly they heard a commotion near the steps. Everyone turned around. But Yakub shouted, "Look forward!"

Benjy peeked. He couldn't help it. He saw a terrorist dragging a man up the stairs. The man was bleeding. A woman was helping the man, holding him up as best she could.

It was the inspector and his wife, Heftzi.

They were pushed toward the front of the cabin. Now everyone could see that Inspector Kohen had been cut across the scalp. His wife had torn some clothing to make a bandage, but the blood was seeping through.

Heftzi saw Benjy and the kids, but tried to avoid eye contact.

Benjy waved a tentative greeting to her, happy to see a familiar face, but Jake quickly leaned over and slapped his hand down. Benjy yelped, "Ouch!" but he got the message.

The inspector, leaning against the bulkhead of the plane, spoke directly to Yakub.

"You people must be insane if you expect to get away with this. No El Al plane has ever been successfully hijacked and this will be no exception."

Yakub just stared at the inspector, not saying a word.

"You really believe you can carry this off?" the inspector continued. He felt himself getting weaker by the minute. Soon he would be in no condition to talk.

"I assume you've noticed you can't even get into the pilot's cabin? The concrete reinforced doors make it a flying fortress. Try to blow it up and you'll only end up blowing a hole in the plane and killing yourselves."

"And the passengers," Yakub added. "No, I don't think your pilot will do much flying without the rest of the plane, wouldn't you agree?" he said smiling.

"But that would be suicide!" the inspector countered. Before he could continue, Jamaya rushed over and kicked the inspector so that he screamed with pain.

"Exactly!" Yakub agreed, holding Jamaya back. "We are willing to die for our cause, are you?"

Yakub spat, turned, and headed for the stairs. He enjoyed seeing the inspector suffer, but he had other things to attend to now.

Jake and Ruth didn't fully understand what was happening. But they understood enough to know Yakub was ready to blow up the entire plane if he didn't get what he wanted.

"What'll we do, Jake?" Ruth whispered.

"I'm thinking," Jake answered, as much in the dark about what to do as she.

"I've got a great plan," Benjy called back.

Both Jake and Ruth shushed him, and ignored him.

"I said I've got a plan," Benjy said, louder this time. Jamaya looked his way.

"What are you saying?" she blared, rushing over to him. Her knife was poised, ready to strike. The little ones started to cry. Ruth tried to quiet them, protecting their trembling bodies with her own. Jake started to talk, knowing that as long as he drew attention to himself, the others would be safe.

"Wh...What did we do?" he asked, loud enough to be heard. Jamaya immediately faced him, knife held high.

"I...I...I mean we're only kids. We can't hurt you. We don't even know what this is about. So, why don't you let us alone?" he pleaded, sweat pouring down his face, his heart pounding what felt like a million times a second.

"Silence!" Jamaya commanded. "No more words from any of you or we kill you all. Understand?"

The children nodded. Jamaya looked at each of them. Ruth tried to cover Rebecca's and Rachel's eyes so they wouldn't start to cry again. Jake quietly prayed.

"Jamaya, come here!" a voice ordered from downstairs. In a flash, she moved toward the steps and disappeared below. Now, all the terrorists were in the coach section of the plane. But, without a plan of action, everyone stayed frozen in place.

Izzy, who was seated behind the blonde woman, kept hearing a humming sound from her direction. It annoyed him because he couldn't make out if it was words or music. Despite their tense situation, Izzy wanted to get to the bottom of it.

He gently tapped the woman on her shoulder. Immediately, the buzzing stopped. She slowly turned around, smiling, her gold tooth clearly visible.

"Er, excuse me, but do you have a radio playing?" Izzy realized how foolish the question sounded, almost as soon as he said it.

"Radio?" she said, in a thick Russian accent. "Nyet. No." But, as she faced forward again, that strange buzzing sound reached his ears again.

"Hey, Jake," Izzy leaned back and whispered. Jake moved forward.

"Not too loud, Izzy, they may come back at any minute. And that Jamaya is really mean."

"Yeah, but there's something strange going on up here."

"Tell me about it," Jake said, sarcastically. "Everything around here is strange, Izzy. What's so different where you're sitting?"

"Well, there's some kind of radio or something up here. It's really weird."

"So?"

"Well, what if the woman in front of me is a spy?"

"Who cares? Whatever is going to happen to us is going to happen to her too."

"Yeah, but — "

"Look, Izzy, just relax. I've got to think of a plan before those guys come back." Jake moved back, hoping something brilliant would come to him. Soon.

He was weighing his options when suddenly he saw the blonde lady stand up in her seat. With one hand she reached up and pulled off her wig, revealing a head of short black hair. Then, with her other hand she reached under her skirt and came out with an AK47 submachine gun.

Benjy, delighted with what he saw, shouted, "See! I knew it! I knew it was a wig!"

Chapter 20
"Kowabanga!"

Jake stood frozen. But as the woman came by, Jake, fearing she might harm the children, grabbed her arm with both hands, and twisted, causing her to yell in pain. The machine gun dropped. But even before it hit the floor, the woman recovered and slapped Jake, hard, so that he crumbled to the floor.

Ruth reached over to help her brother but she was no match for this woman. In a matter of seconds she had pinned Ruth's hands above her head and had a knee in Jake's back. Then, she spoke.

"Listen, you two. I am not a terrorist. I am an Israeli agent who might have been able to go downstairs and do something helpful had you not all decided to declare war on me." She got up, letting go of Ruth's hands and helping Jake up.

"Next time, make sure you know who the enemy is before you declare war. We have little time to lose. Get back to your seats. When the terrorists come up here, take your cues from me. But, don't start anything until I'm ready, understand?"

They rushed to their seats, just as one of the terrorists was coming up the stairs to investigate the commotion. He made his way carefully up the last few steps, his gun the first thing visible in the passageway. The hijacker scanned the cabin for signs of anything unusual. Miraculously, everyone looked normal, that is, scared, which was what the terrorist expected. The Israeli agent had managed to get her wig back on and was seated.

Behind the terrorist came Yakub and Jamaya, ready to do battle. No one made a sound. Faintly, in the background, they could hear Mr. Gold coaching his wife in her breathing technique. The sounds they made alternated between those of a train, "Choo, who, who, choo. Choo, who, who, choo," and something like a stuttering hyena, "Hee, hee, who. Hee, hee, who." Under different circumstances everyone might have thought the sounds quite funny. Right now, no one was laughing.

"What is going on here?" Yakub finally asked, breaking the silence with his sneer.

"You!" he pointed to Abe. "You think I joke when I say do not move? Is that what you think?"

Before Abe could shake his head, Yakub leaped at him and smacked him across the head. Iris, his wife, tried to protect her husband, but succeeded only in getting Yakub angrier. He now began raining blows on both of them.

Rebecca, seeing the fighting, started crying and began calling for her mother. Jake and Ruth tried to quiet her down, but then Rachel began crying too. Benjy, also, started whimpering at the sound of each blow being struck. Pretty soon the younger children were hysterical.

The other male terrorist ran over to the children, preparing to attack. Ruth, seeing him coming, shouted "No-o-o!" and held up her hands to protect the children. The terrorist raised the butt of his gun, ready to strike. All of a sudden he heard a yell, coming from behind him. He turned. But it was too late.

Mr. Gold, hearing his daughter scream, had raced out of the lavatory just in time to see the terrorist preparing to attack Ruth. He leaped, headlong, at the terrorist, bowling him over. They started grappling in the aisle.

Jamaya, seeing her partner in trouble, ran to help him and began pounding and kicking Mr. Gold. Ruth immediately grabbed her hair and pulled with all her might, at the same time whacking the woman in the face with her open palm. Jamaya hit Ruth a glancing blow with her gun, and they both went down.

Yakub stopped hitting Abe and Iris and rushed to help his comrades, shouting, "Stop! Stop! Or I will shoot!" This is what Jake and Izzy were waiting for. As soon as Yakub was close enough, they pounced, forcing him to fall over the writhing bodies on the floor.

Jake was punching as hard as he could, but in such tight quarters it had little effect. Fortunately, for him, the aisle was too narrow for the terrorists to do much harm either.

Izzy decided that the best weapons for him to use were his teeth. He began biting Yakub wherever he could.

Yakub kept yelling, "I will kill you all, aieee! Kill you, aieee! All, aieee!" Each "aieee" indicated that Izzy had found his mark.

Mr. Gold succeeded in pressing his palm against the chin of the terrorist. He kept pushing back harder and harder, forcing the man's head all the way back, almost to his spine.

Benjy saw that his father had pinned his opponent. In one quick motion, he got up on his chair, and shouting his war cry, "Kowabanga!" leaped onto the twitching body of the terrorist.

Mr. Gold, seeing the terrorist was doubled-over in pain, left to help the other children. Benjy, meanwhile, ran back to the armrest, ready for another solo flight onto the terrorist. Again he jumped, and again he shouted, "Kowabanga!" but this time it didn't work out the way he planned. The terrorist, in great pain, but now unhampered by Mr. Gold, was able to crawl away just before Benjy landed. Benjy came down, with all his might, right onto the floor of the cabin. His legs gave way as his knees smashed against his chin. Benjy felt a shooting pain in his head, and was out, cold. The last remaining terrorist, on guard downstairs, came rushing to the scene, gun in hand. There were too many bodies in the aisle for him to do anything from a distance, so he closed in on the trio of Jake, Izzy and Mr. Gold. Yakub was fighting and kicking, occasionally finding his mark on Jake and Izzy. But they were so pumped-up from the battle, they barely felt anything. Each time one of them was pushed away, he would come back, more determined than ever.

In one quick motion, he got up on his chair, and shouting his war cry, "Kowabanga!" leaped onto the twitching body of the terrorist.

The terrorist wasted no time. He grabbed both boys and tossed them, effortlessly, away. With a staggering uppercut he cleared Mr. Gold off Yakub, and then aimed his gun at him.

Jake and Izzy saw the terrorist aim at their father and carefully cock his gun. Mr. Gold, still groggy from the blow, did not realize what was going on. Both boys, in unison, shouted, "Dad, watch out!" but it was too late. A shot shattered the air. All the action in the cabin stopped. Everything froze. Then another shot rang out. And another. The terrorist stared at Mr. Gold, and fell forward...dead.

Standing behind Simon Gold, her wig slightly askew, was the Israeli agent. Her gun still smoking from the shots she had just fired. "Now," she said, "if you will all be so kind as to raise your hands in the air." The terrorists complied. Even Mr. Gold raised his hands, still not clear as to what had happened. Rebecca, seeing her father raise his hands, raised hers too. Rachel, not to be outdone, raised both hands, and one foot.

"Boys," the agent called to Jake and Izzy, "you did a fine job. Although, I distinctly remember telling you to wait for my signal. Please collect their weapons and bring them to me. You," she motioned to Ruth, who had successfully pinned Jamaya early in the battle, "you should be in the Shabak, the Israeli secret service. You were terrific! See if you can help that little one over there to a chair. I think he knocked himself out."

Ruth helped her father pick up Benjy and put him in a chair.

The agent remained quiet for a time, as though concentrating on something. The buzzing noise that Izzy had heard earlier had started again. The agent smiled and, looking at Izzy, said, "Sorry I could not admit to my little transmitter earlier. I'm sure you can understand why. I have been transmitting messages back to Israel almost from the moment the terrorists revealed themselves. If you look out your windows you'll see our fighter planes. They have been alongside for quite some time."

"But weren't you afraid the terrorists might blow up the plane?" Izzy asked.

"We really had no choice. Inspector Kohen had anticipated something of this kind ever since he deciphered your message. Today is the 12th of Ramadan and he knew that a hijacking would take place. The truth is we had teams of agents on every aircraft that left Israel today.

"However, the inspector's plan, if I remember correctly, called for a little less action than what went on here today. Of course, the inspector never mentioned that he had a combat squad like you on the plane with us," she smiled.

Meanwhile, Benjy was slowly coming to his senses. He thought he was on the chair again and shouted, "Kowabanga!" as he awoke. Mr. Gold calmed him down and then went back to his wife.

"The plane has been doing nothing more than circling the airport for almost an hour," the agent said. "Now that the pilot knows everything is under control, we should be landing in about ten minutes."

The two security men went downstairs to tell the passengers what had happened. Soon, the whole coach section was alive with shouting and cheering at the good news.

"All right, everyone," the Israeli agent announced, as she finished tying up the terrorists, "the fasten-safety-belt-sign is lit. Get into your seats." Then looking at Jake and Ruth, she said, "We wouldn't want anyone to fall and hurt themselves."

Everyone laughed, as the plane made its final approach for a landing.

Chapter 21

War Injuries

The waiting room at the Jerusalem Maternity Hospital was filled to bursting. Besides the Gold children, Inspector Kohen, his wife, and two security men, there was an Arab family of five, and a Yemenite family who were busy preparing a meal on the waiting room floor. Cigarette smoke hovered like a cloud above everyone's head and prompted Izzy to deliver a mock weather report of "90 per cent chance of fog inside JM Hospital."

Mr. Gold was in the delivery room with his wife. Naomi had insisted she be taken to Jerusalem to give birth, so that the children could come and visit after school.

The twins were feeling as bad as they looked. Jake had a black eye and a bruised shoulder. Ruth was limping a bit from a swollen ankle and had a big bump on her forehead where the terrorist's gun had grazed her. Izzy had no marks on him, but his tongue was red and swollen. In the heat of battle, he had occasionally bitten it, instead of biting Yakub.

Benjy looked the worst of all. His head was almost completely bandaged. "For my conkuktion," he proudly announced to anyone who would listen. He also had his right arm in a sling because someone had stepped on his hand when he was unconscious. The doctors felt that all Benjy really needed was a bandage for his chin, where he had scraped himself with his knee. But Benjy insisted they give him "the works," complaining that he had a terrible headache, toothache, and chin ache.

The doctors had discounted any concussion, but Benjy nagged them so much they finally agreed to wrapping his head with gauze bandages. "You're right. It's a concussion," they told him with a smile. "Conkuktion," he echoed happily.

Now, Benjy looked like a mummy out for a stroll. He was more than willing to tell everyone about his "war injuries." He had just begun to explain — through hand signals — to one of the Arab children at the hospital how he had beaten up the terrorists, when Mr. Gold burst into the waiting room, and announced, "We have a boy, gang!"

Everyone shouted "Yea!" even Rebecca and Rachel who were busy mooching food off the Yemenite family.

"You can go down to the nursery if you want to see the baby," Mr. Gold told them. The kids flew out.

The inspector and Heftzi congratulated Mr. Gold.

"I know this isn't the time," the inspector whispered, "but as soon as you can, I'd like to see you in my office."

"First thing tomorrow morning," Simon answered, a bit worried. "Or should I come right now?"

"No, tomorrow will be fine. Nine a.m. then. You might want to bring the gang too. And, mazal tov to you all."

Mr. Gold clasped the inspector's outstretched hand. "Thank you for everything," he said. But the inspector's request had cast a shadow over Simon's moment of joy.

Chapter 22
Yea Gang of Four!

Mr. Gold arrived at the police station with the gang of four at 8:45 a.m. The kids had never seen the inside of an Israeli police station and they were anxious to see what Benjy kept calling "the dungeons." They were disappointed when, instead of the heroes' welcome they thought they deserved, they were simply ushered into a small waiting room near the inspector's office.

After a few moments, a door opened and the inspector called to them.

"Come in, Mr. Gold. Sorry if I kept you waiting, but I'm glad you managed to bring the children. Please take a seat," the inspector continued. "Uh, I thought I saw Benjy with you?" Everyone looked out into the hallway. Mr. Gold yelled, "Benjy, where are you?"

"Right here!" Benjy called back, from inside the inspector's office. Sure enough, there was Benjy rolling himself along in the inspector's seat. "Hey gang, look at these great wheels," he called, flying across the room. "I think this seat can do 70 on the highway. Who wants to race?"

Simon glared at his son, leaving little doubt as to what he planned to do to Benjy, and soon.

"Okay, okay," Benjy said as he slid off Inspector Kohen's chair. "The inspector said to take a seat, didn't he?"

"Benjy, you're terrible," Ruth scolded her brother.

Simon turned to the inspector and said, "You wanted to tell us something?"

"Yes. First, the good news. We've captured the entire terrorist cell — Achmed, Yakub and the rest. That Mr. Golan, whom some of you suspected, turned out to be an agent from your own government, sent to watch over you, Mr. Gold. Unfortunately, he and his dog were both wounded by the terrorist who attacked Benjy the first time. Mr. Golan has been in the hospital for most of your...er, adventure.

"As for you kids, I was impressed with how you took care of each other...and the terrorists. You will all receive an award at a ceremony the mayor is going to hold in your honor."

"The gang of four is here to stay," Jake beamed, stretching his hand out. The others ran to put their hands on top of his.

"Yea gang of four!" Ruth shouted.

"Yea gang of four!" the others echoed.

"Please take your seats for a little while longer," the inspector said. "There is more that I have to tell you." He waited for everyone to be seated. "Now for the not-so-good news." Everyone's faces grew grim. "It's not too bad, but I think you should know everything.

"As you know, your father is a rather important man, not only in America but in this country too.

"It seems your father's work in linguistics and his top secret classification make him a prime candidate for terrorists like Yakub and his cell. The Israeli government is studying ways to better insure your father's safety, as well as that of the whole family. But, it is obvious these terrorists received outside help."

"Does all this mean they'll try again?" Izzy asked, a worried look on his face.

"Good question. I only wish we knew the answer. Most likely, they will think many times before starting anything like this again. Naturally, for the next few weeks you'll be getting police protection, but just as a precaution."

Then, trying to create a lighter mood, the inspector said, "Before you know it, your year here will be up and it will be the criminals in America who will be needing protection from your gang of four."

"Maybe we won't even be going back. It would be great to just stay in Israel," Jake wished out loud.

"Well, we'll see," Mr. Gold carefully answered. "For now I think we'd better be getting home, to Jabotinsky Street that is, and start you kids back to school. You don't want to spend next year in the same grade, do you?"

They lined up to shake the inspector's hand and, after getting a grand tour of "the dungeons" the family left. There was a stony silence in the car on the drive back home. The parting words of the inspector echoed in everyone's ears.

"Be careful."

Chapter 23

The Talking Turtle

The Gold family were sitting down for their first quiet meal in days.

Mr. Gold could smell the meatballs simmering on the stove, and his mouth began to water. Naomi had put him on one of those super-strict diets again, absolutely refusing to buy his favorite noshes, despite his pleas. During the days he was home he spent most of his time at the computer. He had all too few opportunities to leave the house to "stock up" at Seraph's, his favorite bakery. But, early that morning, Simon had managed to sneak a few chocolate cream-filled cookies into the house when he went to buy a newspaper.

Unfortunately, Simon was not the only one in the house with a sweet tooth. Little Rachel lost no time in finding his hiding place and helping herself to his treasure. After she had stuffed herself, she waddled into his office, her face covered with chocolate, and a giant cookie partially crumbled in each hand. She had decided to share.

"Oh, no!" Simon moaned, genuinely upset. His wife, hearing her husband's pained cry, rushed into his room, not knowing what to expect. She was more than a little surprised to find Simon trying to coax their one-year-old daughter into giving him what was left of his cookies.

"Topper," Naomi scolded, "look at you. A grown man trying to take cookies from a baby. Aren't you ashamed? Stealing Rachel's cookies!"

"Her cookies? What do you mean her cookies? Those are mi — " Mr. Gold suddenly remembered his diet.

"Go ahead, Topper, those are what?"

"Those are mighty fine-looking cookies for a little kid to eat, don't you think?" he answered, feeling just a little foolish at having to lie about his cookies.

"You know, sometimes you are such a baby. I know very well those are your cookies and I'm glad Rachel found them. I've been looking all over for them myself. Don't think I didn't see you sneak them in between the folds of your newspaper. Honestly, for a computer genius you act like such a child sometimes." Naomi glared at her husband. In one swift motion, she picked up Rachel, gooey hands and all, and stormed out of the room.

"Well, who wants to start by telling me their day?" Simon asked, using the traditional opening. "But no talk about terrorists, kidnappers or secret messages, okay?" He got no argument from anyone.

"Okay, Jacob, why don't you begin? What kind of a day did you have today?"

"Interesting."

"What kind of interesting?" Mr. Gold prompted, hoping this wouldn't turn into one of those teeth-pulling sessions.

"Well, the teacher went on army reserve duty today, so we had a substitute."

"And?" It was going to be one of those sessions. Just when he had caught a glimpse of the brown rice with mushrooms, one of his favorite side-dishes.

"And that made it very interesting," Jake said with a smile.

"Well, you can't beat that for an interesting day," Simon said, happy to give up. "Why don't we move on to Ruth now?" he quickly snuck in, hoping his wife wouldn't notice.

She did.

"Dear," Mrs. Gold took over. "Jacob obviously has something more to tell us, don't you, Jacob?"

"Okay, Mom, but I don't think you'll like it."

"You know I try not to be judgmental. I'm sure I can accept whatever you have to say."

"Keep it clean," his father whispered under his breath.

"Well, when the substitute came in we discovered it was a woman! Can you imagine a woman substitute? She didn't have a chance!" Everyone leaned closer to the table now, especially the children. They knew this was going to be good.

"But you only have men teachers in your school, don't you, Jacob? I mean, that is the rule, isn't it?" His mother had a bad feeling about this story.

"You're right, Mom. We only have men teachers. At

least we did, until this lady walked in. I don't think she understood what was going to happen either. I mean, the school must have asked for a substitute teacher and whoever it is that sends substitutes must have thought the girls' school had called. Anyway, once she was in the class it was too late for her to leave. Besides, the kids had already blocked the exit."

"They did what?" This whole story was getting more and more improbable by the minute. "Is this one of those Benjy karate stories, Jacob?" his mother asked.

"Hey," Benjy called out from the other end of the table, "I didn't do anything. Leave me outta this."

"I'm sorry, Benjamin," his mother apologized. "Go ahead, Jacob."

"Now, it gets really interesting."

"Did they hit her?" Benjy asked. "Ugh, girls! I bet they slammed her good."

"Benjamin!" his mother warned. "As you suggested, we prefer to leave you out of this."

"No. No one hit her," Jacob continued. "But, just as she was opening her lesson plan to begin to teach, everyone started leaving."

"You too?" his mother asked, disappointed.

"No, I stayed."

"Good boy!" she applauded.

"Teacher's pet!" Benjy taunted.

"And what did you say to her?" Mrs. Gold prompted.

"Nothing. I just watched her cry."

"Cry?" Ruth broke in. "Why did she cry? She should have grabbed those kids and brought them back into class."

"Well, that's all she did, cry," Jake said again, looking at his sister.

"And then?" his mother asked.

"Then I walked up to her and asked her if she was all right. She said yes and that this was only her second substitute job and she didn't know what to do. I told her not to worry because we sometimes walk out on our regular teacher too. That seemed to make her feel better. She thanked me, dried her eyes and asked my name. Then, I left too."

"You mean you sometimes walk out on your regular teacher?" Mrs. Gold began wondering what kind of school she was sending her son to.

"No, of course not, Mom. Mr. Kreshstone would kill us if we tried that. But, I thought it would make her feel better if I lied a little. So, I did."

"You're okay, Jake," his father said.

"That was nice of you, Jacob, even if you did lie." His mother was a bit more reserved in her praise. Lying, even for the best of reasons, could not be encouraged.

"Now, how about you, Ruth?" Simon began again. "What have you to report?"

"Um, let me see. Remember the math test that was set for next Tuesday?"

"Sure, we've got a tutor coming tonight and Monday night to help you out."

"Well, I won't need him," Ruth announced.

"You mean you understand the work?" her mother asked.

"Not exactly. It's just that I got things a bit mixed up.

It's the history test we have next Tuesday. The math test was today."

"How did it go?" Mr. Gold asked, a tentative smile on his face. Math was not Ruth's best subject. Math — in Hebrew — was her worst.

"I think I did pretty well," Ruth answered, sounding very confident.

"That's wonderful, Ruth," her mother beamed, "I knew you would catch on eventually."

"Yep, this was the first time I understood all the questions in Hebrew. I didn't even have to ask the teacher to help me with the big words."

"Wonderful! Wonderful!" Mr. Gold knew what a struggle math could be. It had never been his best subject either. "So, you think you did pretty good. I'm really proud, Ruthy."

"Well, I would have done pretty good, I think, except that by the time I finished reading and understanding the questions, the test was over. So, I don't think I got too high a mark."

"So what?" Mrs. Gold said.

"Yes, who cares?" Simon seconded. "I still can't read a Hebrew newspaper, and I probably wouldn't have been able to read the math questions, let alone answer them. Why, if I had to take that test I — "

"Okay, Dad I get the picture. You don't want me to feel bad. Don't worry, I don't."

Simon hated it when his children undermined his attempts at child psychology. Ruth, in particular, always seemed to know what he was thinking.

It's not enough I married a social worker, I raised one as well, he thought to himself.

"And now you, Benjy," he said out loud. "What kind of day did you have, or shouldn't I ask?"

"Oh, no, you can ask, Dad." Benjy always took his father seriously. "I had a big fight today," he announced.

"Oh, no," his mother said. "Why, why must you always be fighting?"

"Well, it wasn't just me, Mom. It was Yosef, my friend, too."

"Are you sure you want to hear this?" Simon asked his wife. He was certain that Benjy was setting them up for another tall tale. Normally, he would sit back and try to enjoy it, but those meatballs were calling, and his stomach was responding.

"You mean you were defending your friend?" Naomi chose to ignore her husband's remark. To her anything the children had to say was important.

"Sort of."

"What do you mean, 'sort of,' Benjamin?" asked Mr. Gold.

"It was like this, see. Yosef had a pet turtle — "

"I knew it!" Simon banged on the table. "I knew he was going to do this to me. You're going to tell us about a karate-chopping turtle, aren't you? One of those Ninja turtles, no doubt. Well, let me — "

"Simon," his wife scolded, "let him finish."

"No, Dad," Benjy continued, "this is no karate-choppin' turtle. Yosef has a turtle that talks. And he says things like, 'How are you?' in Hebrew of course. And only to people he likes. Yosef brought him into school, but Yoel said that no turtle can speak, no way. Of course, I'm Yosef's friend and when I say 'hi' to the turtle he always asks how I am. So, I said to Yoel that the turtle didn't like him and that's why he wouldn't talk to him. So Yoel said I should say 'hi' to the turtle and he would see if it could talk. But Yosef said that the turtle would never talk in front of a baby like Yoel. And then we had a fight."

How does he do it? Simon thought. Then he said, "Let me get this sort of straight, Benjy. You had a fight over a supposedly talking turtle?"

"Yeah, a real supposedly talking turtle," Benjy insisted.

"You had this fight just because Yoel didn't believe the turtle could talk?" his mother added.

"No. Not because of that. Because of what Yoel did after Yosef called him a baby."

"What did he do?" Simon suddenly realized he had fallen into Benjy's trap. Again.

"He grabbed the turtle from Yosef and threw him out the window."

"Yosef?" Izzy gasped.

"No, the turtle."

"And then you had the fight?" Naomi asked.

"Yep. Because Yosef was afraid of Yoel, so I hit Yoel for him."

"I can understand that, Benjamin," Mr. Gold sighed, hoping this was the end of the story. "It's good you stuck up for your friend."

"Yep, and then I hit Yosef."

"What?" everyone at the table said at once.

"Sure, he started hitting me for hitting Yoel."

"Wait a minute," Simon pleaded. "I thought you were helping Yosef against Yoel?"

"Yeah, but Yosef was angry at me for hitting his brother."

"What brother?" Izzy chimed in.

"His brother Yoel who threw the turtle out the window." Benjy said it slowly so that even Izzy would understand.

Mrs. Gold knew she was beaten.

"My goodness, Benjy, you certainly had a rough day. Did you all make up?"

"Yep."

"That's nice, dear." Naomi secretly wondered what her brother, the psychiatrist, would say about talking turtles. She decided, for her own sake, not to ask him.

"Thanks, Mom." Benjy stood up from the table, searching for something. "And here's the turtle. They gave it to me. Look," he said, putting the turtle on the table, "he even walks — a little. Although before Yoel threw him out the window he used to walk much faster. But I'm still a little sad."

"About what?" his mother asked, after she overcame her initial fright at seeing the turtle on the table.

"Well, he stopped talking. Completely!" Benjy sounded totally dejected.

After a moment of silence, first Jake, then Ruth, and then everyone, started laughing. Benjy was very insulted and, stuffing his turtle back in his pocket, sat down.

"I'm sorry, Benjy," Mr. Gold apologized, "but who knows, maybe he just has a bad case of laryngitis after all the talking he's done lately. If we get him on our medical plan, I'm sure we can get someone to fix him up as good as new."

"Hey, could we?" Benjy asked, starting everyone in a peal of laughter again.

"Enough, Topper," his wife said, also laughing. "It's okay Benjy. You can take care of the turtle, but please wash your hands now. You certainly can't eat at the table when you've just touched a turtle."

Benjy was glad to get away from the table. He felt no one ever really believed him. He was almost right.

"Well, that leaves only you, Izzy," Mr. Gold smiled. "But, I doubt you'll be able to beat that one."

"My day was serious, Dad," Izzy began. "I tried to tell my teacher about what happened to us and how come I'm so far behind in my work, but he wouldn't listen to me."

"Well, if that's all, don't worry. I'll write you a note tomorrow confirming everything and asking him to excuse you until you have a chance to make it up. But you've got to work hard, understand?" Simon felt glad that he could solve at least one problem.

"Thanks, Dad, but it's more than that."

"Naturally." Simon wondered if it would be possible for him to take his meals in his room from now on.

"It's just that I keep feeling I'm being followed. Every time I walk to school I think someone is following me."

"Isaac," Naomi said, taking over from her husband. "You spoke to the inspector. You know all the terrorists are either dead or safely locked away in jail. There's no one to hurt you, Isaac. You are absolutely safe." She

"Look," he said, putting the turtle on the table, "he even walks
— a little. Although before Yoel threw him out the window he
used to walk much faster."

looked him straight in the eyes. "You believe me, don't you?"

"I want to Mom, but that feeling doesn't go away." He was silent a moment. "I know there's nothing to be afraid of, and I'm going to try and get over it."

"After all," Simon added, "it just doesn't make sense that someone would just be following you and not the rest of us. Why would he choose you over, let's say, Benjy, who runs around by himself everywhere? And certainly no one could get in here with all the alarms and locks we've put in since this whole mess ended. Why, I — "

"I didn't say I was scared to be in the house," Izzy lied.

"We know you're not afraid, Izzy." Naomi assured him. "But even if you were, there's nothing wrong with that. It's only wrong not to ask for help to work out your fears." There was a deep note of sympathy in her voice. It embarrassed her son.

Isaac's eyes started to water and he excused himself from the table.

"See what you did?" Mrs. Gold accused her husband.

"Me? I was trying to help him over — "

"Well, that's not the way to do it," his wife shot back, before he could finish his sentence. Without saying another word she got up to serve the meal.

"Why do I feel I'm constantly being interrupted?" Simon said to no one in particular. "Don't answer that," he warned Benjy as he was about to answer.

Rebecca raised her hand.

"What is it now, Rebecca?" Mr. Gold grumbled, still upset.

"You didn't ask me?"

"Okay, Rebecca, what happened to you today?" There was no reason to let it out on the children, he thought to himself. He tried to smile. It was slow in coming.

"I gave Rachel her medicine," Bekka answered proudly.

"That's nice, Bekka. Which medicine?"

"I gave her three of these medicines," she announced, holding up three small stones.

"You gave her three stones to eat?" Mr. Gold felt himself tensing up again.

"Oh, no," she calmly answered. "I didn't give her stones."

"Thank God," Mr. Gold sighed.

"I gave her pebbles!"

"Naomi!" Simon yelled into the kitchen. Naomi was just serving the meatballs. The panicky sound of her husband's voice startled her, causing her to spill some hot gravy on her hand. She yelled "Ouch!" and rushed out of the kitchen, still carrying the serving spoon.

"What? What is it?" she asked.

"Rebecca just told me she fed Rachel three stones today." Simon sounded frantic.

"No I didn't," Rebecca insisted. "I gave her pebble medicine."

"What should we do?" Mr. Gold asked helplessly. The other children were concerned too, especially Benjy who was trying to pry open Rachel's mouth to look for the pebbles. Rachel kept shouting. "No!" and smacking him with her Mickey Mouse spoon.

"Is that all?" Naomi said, anger rising within her. "That's what you got me half burned to death for?"

"But isn't it serious?" Simon asked, wondering why his wife wasn't concerned. He was usually the calm one during a crisis.

"No, it's not serious! I found the four pebbles when I diapered her earlier. I told Rebecca not to do it again. Right, Bekka?"

Rebecca nodded.

"Four pebbles?" Mr. Gold turned to Rebecca.

"Yes," she answered, "she liked the pebble medicine so much she took one herself. But I told her she was gonna get a belly ache because she took one of the stones and not one of the pebbles."

"Of course." Simon had such a look of exasperation on his face that everyone, including his wife, started to laugh.

Naomi went back to the kitchen and returned with a giant plate of meatballs, spaghetti, and rice with mushrooms. Simon tried to take some. "That's not for you, dear," Naomi told him. She went back to the kitchen and came back with a large bowl filled with raw vegetables. "Diet," she said.

Simon wished they had a dog. Even a cat. Anything that would eat his vegetables for him. For a brief second he thought about the turtle, but realized it would take too long.

"Remember, Topper, you've still got another ten pounds to lose," his wife called as she went to check on their newest addition. "And remember, no cheating!"

Simon looked at the meatballs. At the mushrooms with

rice. At his children digging in. He was trying to remember what his wife had said.

"I'll remember tomorrow," he whispered under his breath. Content, he lifted the plate of meatballs and heaped a large portion onto his soggy salad.

"Nothing like a bed of meatballs," Simon announced, smiling at the children as they looked up from their plates.

"Dig in," he prompted, as they all smiled back.

THE GANG OF FOUR
WANTS YOU
TO WRITE!

Ruth, Jake, Izzy and Benjy (Kapow!) would love to hear from you. So if you would like to write to them and tell them how you enjoyed reading about their adventures, please do.

The Gang of Four can be reached by writing:
> The Gang of Four
> POB 4636
> Jerusalem, Israel 91044